ALWAYS

Stephanie Roberts

ISBN: 978-0-6485363-6-9

Stephanie Roberts/Author Wyoming, Gosford, NSW 2250
For Hardcover Coffee Table version or any other paperbacks not available on Amazon, write to:

stephanieroberts@iinet.net.au to order direct.

Facebook Author, Writer & Tarot Pages:
https://www.facebook.com/StephanieRobertsAuthor/
https://www.facebook.com/StephanieRobertsWriter
https://www.facebook.com/stephaniemarietarot

Website: for all Books and Tarot Reading:
https://stephaniemarietarot.com/

Dedicated to my husband Chris, who has journeyed through life with me.
Every passing day we walk in unison, not allowing life's challenges to wither away the special feeling for each other, embedded deep in our hearts and souls.
~ Stephanie

Quotation

There is a sacredness in tears. They are not the mark of weakness, but of power. They speak more eloquently than ten thousand tongues. They are the messengers of overwhelming grief, of deep contrition, and of unspeakable love. *~ Washington Irving*

CONTENTS

THE END

How, she wonders, will their story end?

It is autumn in Australia on the beautiful central coast in the town of Gosford. The year is 1999. She sits by her study window, looking out into the courtyard. Harry, her husband, has a green thumb—probably green fingers too, all eight of them. The rain always makes the garden look brighter. Harry's garden is magical, a combination of exotic and classical species, ever-blooming and lush all year round. A collection of multi-coloured shrubs and eye-popping plants, beautiful blooms of geranium, white peace lily and red anthurium. The central focus is Virginia, elegantly detailed, holding a lotus flower in her upstretched hands from which a gentle cascade of water flows over her female form.

The birds who have made the garden their home splash and frolic in the fountain as it flows into the water bowl at Virginia's feet. This is Georgia's little slice of heaven viewed from her window. Billy, the red wattle bird, is 'chok choking' at her window, waiting for his noodles. Yes, noodles. Not pasta or rice but his favourite two-minute noodles—with cheese. Jack and Jill, the rainbow lorikeets, come up to the window to join him, asking her to come out and spread the usual scraps of grain-bread on the patch of grass under the fountain. And Buddy, the white cockatoo, is on his perch, impatiently waiting for the seed tray to be filled, screeching for attention.

There is a slight drizzle and the air is chilly. She is a sight this morning: t-shirt and hooded sweatshirt, a warm vest under both of those and flannel pants, old thick socks—one with a hole in it. She has the heating turned up and the vent over her head is blowing hot air onto the hair piled up on her head in an untidy twisted bun. She has always been one to feel the cold, even at a young age, having been born in a tropical country. Her hometown of Bangalore, India, has a tropical climate. Even in the winter months of December to February, the temperature does not go below 16°. Now, at fifty-five years, she accepts her age and she is grateful for her healthy body, fitness of mind and zest for life, even though her body feels colder!

Reflecting on her life from the age of seven, she is grateful for the years gone by. She has ridden the roller-coaster of life without fear of the unknown, taking on every challenge head on from a young age, due to the circumstances of her life. She is not bitter over those circumstances. Some pain and hurt lingers as they come to mind, on and off, but less so now. Mostly due to the wonderful man that has stood by her side for a lifetime.

Today is the 6th of May. The day of her wedding in 1969—thirty years ago. Not a day of great significance, and one that is filled with bittersweet memories. But wait till you hear her story.

Georgia arrives at the hospital. The African nurse gives her a dazzling smile, almost blinding her with her sparkling white teeth. What it is to be twenty-one and have your whole life ahead of you! She will have an exceptional one with a smile like hers. 'Go right in, Mrs Haines,' she says. Her eyes contradict her smile and hold a sympathy only a compassionate human being can have.

The nurses, day-care staff and receptionist find her a familiar face, having walked the hospital corridor for the last three weeks. They all have bright smiles and cheery greetings to offer, but the whispers as she passes them would probably be 'that poor lady', 'she hopes every day will bring a change'.

Harry is a competitive workaholic, planning and conducting events for a large government department. It is secret work, coordinating with the federal police and the Department of Foreign Affairs on expected terrorist attacks.

At least he enjoys his work, which is more than most of his colleagues can say, she thinks.

Her husband is a man of few words, but she knows he loves her dearly, even though she often complains that he is not romantic. When she asks how much he loves her, he usually replies with something silly, like, 'One thumbnail only.'

They argue about everything, it seems, but her mother-in-law always said, 'When two people argue, it doesn't mean they *don't* love each other; and when they don't argue, it doesn't mean they *do* love each other.'

Wise woman, Mother Meg. For thirty years she was a surrogate mum to Georgia, and not at all like the stereotypical mother-in-law. Her girlfriends couldn't believe she adored her husband's mother; they had nothing but complaints about theirs. Mother Meg died too young, only seventy-two years old.

Georgia felt she had lost the one person in her life who utterly understood her.

Harry's life hangs like a thread. He has been in a coma for three weeks.

Entering the room and walking up to the hospital bed, Georgia's heart overflows with love and compassion for this man—her husband.

Her psychic friend, Mariah, said, 'We weave the tapestry of our cloth on earth with threads of heart, energy and will. Our way in life starts and ends with heart. When the heart energy isn't flowing, arterial blockage and heart attack occurs.'

As Harry sleeps, she begins to write, pouring out her heart in the first love letter to her husband of thirty years.

My Dearest Harry,

When you said, 'You are a part of me,' I didn't reply. I want to tell you now, you are in me.

Looking down the tunnel of our love, I haven't told you enough how much you mean to me. It would seem I have taken for granted all those years that you have loved me unconditionally.

You have been my mother, father, brother, sister, husband, lover, and best friend, all rolled into one. A man who has seen me mature from a young seventeen-year-old to the woman I am today. You have stood by me through thick and thin: my tantrums, success and loss in business, and the heartbreak over the passing of my doggie sons.

You accepted that I could not have children after the tragic loss of our first son and never laid blame. Instead you loved me more, if that was even possible. You lived your life for me, through me and with me.

Nothing you did for me was ever a chore.

You gave your life to us—me, and all the furry kids. I often called you my 'pack horse'. You have carried me all my life. Everything I am today, you have taught me, not by telling, but by shining example. You are my guardian angel. My Rock.

With you I have experienced an awesome adventure that has taken me into the deep recesses of my heart and opened doors I never knew existed. I discovered the hidden power within myself. In the languages of the world, there are countless references to the feelings of the heart.

Over the years, I came to realise these feelings contain within them a power to seek, to understand, to do. You have helped me unravel an understanding of this untapped source of energy within myself. I have realised that heart-power is the electricity of my inner strength and potential. It's what gives me the self-motivated ability to manifest and complete goals, to empower, and to achieve balance and fulfilment, even in today's increasingly stressful world.

Thirty years have passed since we met, playing 'the honeymoon game'.

Youth is not a time of life; it is a state of mind, it's a temper of will, a quality of the imagination, a vigour of the emotions. It is a freshness of the deep springs of life. Nobody grows old by merely living a number of years; people grow old by deserting their ideals and dreams.

You are etched in my heart forever.

Georgia

Folding the letter, she puts it neatly in an envelope with his name and stands it against the glass of water on the bedside table.

Is this where their story ends? Maybe, just maybe, it will go on—just a bit longer.

HARRY

Harry was born to Sean and Meg Haines, the middle child of a family of five, in Pallavaram, a locality in Chennai, Tamil Nadu, India, towards the end of the Second World War. As the middle child, Harry often felt alone because the other four siblings paired up, being closer in age. Much to the annoyance of his brothers, Harry managed to get away with any escapade, unscathed by his parents' wrath. However, being a loner would stand him in good stead later in life.

Sean was the son of a British officer stationed in India. Meg was the daughter of a French army officer stationed in Pondicherry. Pondicherry was one of the eight union territories of former French India. Sean worked for the local Post and Telegraph Office. His salary was very modest, and the family survived on the bare necessities.

Meg was a part-time French teacher for the local school. When Harry was six years old his father secured a welcome promotion in his job to that of Postmaster in the city of Bangalore, and the family moved to the big city, the beautiful garden city of India in the late fifties.

The gentle climate of this city and the perfect amalgamation of the sun and the rain provided an ideal environment for sustaining the greenery. The occasional heat waves were cooled frequently by thunderstorms. This pattern maintained a balance and encouraged the growth of mini-forests, providing tree cover for the entire city. Young Harry had a passion for plants and birds and couldn't wait to explore this picturesque place. His brothers, on the other hand, were not even slightly interested in gardens and headed for Bangalore city's nightclubs and discos.

Harry spent hours wandering in the famous botanical garden, Lal Bagh, also known as the Red Garden, established in the 1760s. Originally the Cypress Garden, it was internationally famous and drew much attention due to its rare collection of plant species from the entire Indian subcontinent. Many wildlife species called Lal Bagh their home: the myna birds, parakeets, Brahmini kites and many more. Lotus pools, fountains and lush green lawns were spread through about 240 acres in this enchanting garden.

The boys were sent to a Protestant school, Baldwin Boys High School. Though the family were of the Catholic faith, the headmaster at the Protestant school gave Papa Sean a discount on school fees for the five boys. The Catholic school would not allow this discount.

Harry was happy at Baldwin High and excelled in all subjects, especially mathematics, and was often set assignments that were given to senior students. When he finished his final exam in twenty minutes, and left the exam hall to sit on the steps of the school, his maths teacher, Mr Ramachandran, reprimanded him. 'Harry, it's an hour-long paper. Have you completed it?'

'Yes, sir, I'm done.'

'Did you *not* know some of the answers?' his teacher asked in astonishment.

'Answered them all, sir.'

Harry maxed his paper—100%.

He was a keen sportsman and participated in every sport on the school curriculum: swimming, hockey, soccer, cricket, athletics, and boxing. He excelled at most sports but had a passion for boxing.

Harry's interest in sport led to two events that would influence the rest of his life.

The first event was a visit to his school by a team of 'footballers' from Australia. These footballers played a game of football known as the Victorian Football League, which was unlike any other game that young Harry had ever seen. His eyes shone with excitement as he watched the players.

In 1958 players from the Premiership winning team in the Victorian Football League (VFL)—the Collingwood Football Club—visited India and played a number of exhibition games at the Baldwin Boys High School. Fifteen-year-old Harry was eager to learn more about this strange game and soon made friends with Australian rules footballer Michael John 'Mick' Twomey. Through this friendship, Harry learned as much as he could about football, Collingwood, the VFL and Australia.

After the games he sat with Mick on the school steps when everyone had left and came to an understanding about the land Down Under—the world's smallest continent and largest island: Australia, a paradise.

Harry was fascinated by Mick's stories about Australia's quirky wildlife, its coral reefs, picturesque rain forests, stunning beaches, and scorching deserts, and his revered tales of the aboriginal tribes. A land of staggering contrasts and spectacular beauty.

Mick pulled out snapshots he had taken on his box Brownie camera of the kangaroos and koalas, Australia's native animals.

'I can't wait to get there,' Harry said, jumping up with excitement.

Mick clapped him on the back and tousled the young lad's hair. He was the kind of nice guy that encouraged young boys to accomplish their goals.

Harry soaked up knowledge about Australia. The outback, rugged national parks and red-earthed deserts sounded particularly adventurous to a young boy. It was topped off with Mick telling him that 'Aussies' were a laid-back and friendly people.

'Australia, here I come,' yelled Harry, beside himself.

'Meet up Down Under, mate. See you on the team!'

The second event occurred two years later, just as Harry was completing his leaving school certificate.

At around the same time a young fella in the US was attracting headline stories for his successes in the boxing ring. His name was Cassius Clay. He was approximately the same age as Harry. Clay won his first bout in 1954. He went on to win the Golden Gloves tournament for novices in 1956 and the Olympic Gold in 1960. Immediately after he won the Olympic Gold he turned professional. Newspapers loved him from day one and he was a hero even before he turned professional. He was Harry's idol.

Harry's prowess in boxing attracted the attention of the father of one of the other students at the school, Wing Commander Sunit Razdan, Indian Air Force. The officer was impressed by Harry's performance in the boxing competition finals and invited him to participate in an exhibition bout at the air force base in Dehradun in Northern India.

He had no hesitation accepting the invitation, much to the apprehension of his parents, especially his mother, who did not think he would come out of the boxing match alive.

Harry was thrilled to be transported from Bangalore to Dehradun Air Force Base in a Douglas Dakota military plane. He was made to feel very welcome at the air force base. On arrival he was allocated living quarters in the officers' quarters and dined in the officers' mess.

A flight cadet by the name of Anil Kumar took Harry on a tour of the gymnasium and facilities.

'So ya fighting the big one, Harry? The wing commander's son?'

Harry contained his surprise and asked nonchalantly, 'What are you training for, Anil?'

'Hope to be commissioned to be a fighter pilot,' Anil replied, all fired-up. 'The de Havilland Vampire fighter-bomber—that's the mean machine I wanna fly!'

As they entered the gym, a boy, about six feet tall, muscles bulging out of his white t-shirt, was leaving and said hello to Anil.

'Hey, champ, come and meet someone,' Anil said.

The boy stopped.

'Sunil, this is Harry. He's your opponent in the ring.'

The boy looked at Harry. A long hard look.

Harry was the first to extend his hand, which was grabbed in a vice and shaken enthusiastically. Sunil's grin showed a row of even white teeth. None had been knocked out.

'Good to meet ya Harry boy. See ya in the first round, probably not much more—alive.'

And the big one turned and sauntered off.

The day arrived and they stepped into the ring. It was to be a three-round bout.

In the first round they tested each other, jabs and blocks. They explored each other's strengths and weaknesses. Sunil feinted and landed a good blow on Harry's ribs, but the follow-up, a hook to Harry's jaw, caught air as Harry astutely pulled his head back. A stupid mistake, Harry thought, but it was gone from his mind in a moment. His coach always said, 'Dwell on the past, you'll die in the present.'

The second round was more physical and both boxers fared well.

Now was the time to pay attention. Don't lose a tick, watch for that dropped guard, keep your eyes on the prize. Be patient, take your hits; pretty boy will make a mistake.

Third round, three minutes in, and the hulk made his mistake. His first mistake. And his last.

When he threw a punch, Harry deflected Sunil's arm, which caused him to turn slightly to his right and expose the left side of his jaw. Light-footed and agile, Harry moved at lightning speed and landed a mighty blow on the jaw, downing his opponent.

The in-ring referee commenced the count, '1-2-3 … 8-9-10.'

Sunil remained down for the count, and, as abruptly as that, the bout ended.

Harry, with only a bloody nose, emerged victorious and elated. He had defeated the wing commander's son.

The hulk was a good sport and they were to become fast friends in due course.

On the flight back from Dehradun to Bangalore the pilot invited Harry into the cockpit, seated in a collapsible seat known as the jump seat. It was a real buzz for the boxing champion to be travelling in the cockpit of the aircraft on such a long flight.

An indelible memory for the fifteen-year-old.

Sunil's grandfather, Andrew Caves, a retired air marshal, was impressed with Harry, and not just because of his physical boxing prowess. He saw in him a lad with the staying power and dedication to go far in life. He would later remember Harry and offer him employment in his stockbroking business.

In Bangalore, India, in the 1950s, there were no public swimming pools.

Children, therefore, swam in the local wells. These wells, constructed inland, were used to irrigate crops. Farmhands climbed down the stairwell to the water level twenty to thirty feet below surface and filled brass urns with the water, which they then carried skilfully on their heads to the fields.

Not far from Harry's home in Richmond Town, Bangalore, was a palm orchard which contained a number of these wells. Palm trees were tapped to make toddy, a favourite drink of the Indian people.

Harry persuaded his brothers to help him learn to swim.

A rope was tied around Harry's waist. The swimming lesson consisted of lowering the learner into the water, leaving sufficient slack to allow him to 'swim' as best he could through trial and error. Without drowning.

The older boys became engrossed in their game of cricket and forgot about Harry tied to the slack rope left on the edge of the well and secured by a rock.

Harry's lifeline gave away, and he found himself sputtering underwater. Panicking and unable to surface, he was sure his end had arrived.

Fortunately one of the boys tripped on the rope and raised the alarm.

Jeremy, his elder brother, instinctively sat on Harry's chest, forcing him to discharge the water filling his lungs.

He was green around the gills for a long time. Mother Meg reprimanded him and his brothers severely, but she was secretly relieved he had not drowned. She was never sure what scrapes her fifteen-year-old would get into next.

His near drowning experience did not deter young Harry, who progressed rapidly in learning to swim and dive and went on to win competitions in underwater swimming and high-board diving.

He would now be able to have a blast, snorkelling and diving in the ocean waters of the island continent, Australia, he had heard so much about from his footballer friend, Mick Twomey.

On 15 August 1947, India ceased to exist as a British colony. In its place were created two separate sovereign states, India and Pakistan.

At this time in India, most of the British troops had withdrawn and government had passed into the hands of the Indian people.

During the time of the British Raj in India a new group of people with mixed British and Indian ancestry grew, commonly referred to as Anglo-Indians.

It was estimated that approximately two million people living in India were Anglo-Indian. During the Indian Independence Movement, it was generally felt that Anglo-Indians identified with British rule and they incurred the hostility of the Indian people. Anglo-Indians were desperate to flee India at all costs. Those who could afford the fare by boat or plane left immediately bound for Britain, Canada, Australia, and other countries. Others who were not so financial found ingenious ways of making the journey. The favoured option for students and young people was to secure employment on a cruise liner as a deck hand or cleaner to enable them to reach the shores of Britain. The more adventurous opted to travel by push bike from India to Calais and take a ferry to Dover. This migration out of India continued for years.

Many of Harry's fellow students decided to leave by any means possible. His group of friends, at the age of fifteen, rode on bicycles to France and boarded a ship to the UK. In those days, if you could make it to England you could adopt the country as your home.

These options were not available to Harry—he had no money and he did not own a push bike. But mostly he did not want to go to Britain or Canada.

Australia was his vision.

Harry developed a plan to accomplish his ultimate goal. He attained a job with the Post and Telegraph Office as a telegraphist. He worked extra shifts and as many hours of overtime as the office permitted him and saved every *rupee* out of what was left of his meagre wage after he gave most of it to his mother to help with food rations and clothing for the family.

As schoolboys, his elder brother received the new clothing and shoes which were eventually handed down to Harry, as third in line, usually threadbare and leather worn.

Harry did not mind and walked to school barefoot, quite buoyantly. However, he liked to tease his mother.

'Why do I *always* have to have old raggedy clothes and worn-out shoes, Mum? Don't you love me?'

These words would bring tears to his mother's eyes and Harry would pull her hair, plant a kiss on her cheek, and run away with a smile.

As luck would have it, the retired air marshal, Andrew Caves, whom Harry had met on his trip to Dehradun, had settled in Bangalore and commenced business as a stockbroker. He remembered the zealous lad who had left a lasting impression on him.

One afternoon his mother handed him the envelope that arrived in the post, with the distinguished Indian Air Force Squadron crest.

'Why is the air force writing to you, my son? Have you applied to join the forces?' she asked tentatively with worry in her eyes.

Tearing the envelope open, Harry read the letter, written in a penmanship so neat it almost seemed like calligraphy, and shouted excitedly, 'No, Mum, but I have been offered a position of office manager with the retired air force officer, Andrew Caves, who I met over a year ago, in his stockbroking business.'

When Harry explained the whys and wherefores of the need to work at two jobs, Andrew Caves came to an agreement with Harry. He would work the daylight hours at his office, and keep his post at the Telegraphs Office.

'Admirable, son,' Andrew Caves said, slapping Harry on the back. 'Work for me for a year and I will pay your fare to Australia in lieu of a wage.'

This would amount to much more than Harry could earn in a year as an office manager in those days. Harry was taken aback at this unexpected generous offer and was quick to accept. The stockbroker and his new office manager shook hands, and the deal was made.

Securing a permanent resident's visa to Australia was yet another unnerving challenge. The application process for migrant positions to Australia was extremely competitive and consisted of a written application followed by a rigorous face-to-face interview with the trade commissioner at the time. Harry was required to attend this interview accompanied by his entire family. His parents thought it was a waste of time. No boy with his impoverished background would be accepted for migration to a foreign country, they said.

His brothers mocked him. 'You, raggedy boy, going to Australia? What will you do there? Shine shoes?'

'You don't have any money to get there anyway,' said his elder brother Jeremy. 'Do you plan to rob a bank?'

But Harry had the fare. He had worked two jobs day and night: at his post and telegraphs job at the General Post Office through the night till the early hours of the morning; snatching a few hours' sleep before arriving at the stockbroker's office, where he learnt the business of the stock exchange and good customer service.

Harry also had to provide evidence of financial support by a sponsor in Australia. The selection process openly favoured applicants who had a tertiary qualification, some working experience, and a viable financial sponsor.

Harry's first application was rejected. He did not have the third requirement, a viable financial sponsor.

Taking his fountain pen and the best sheet of foolscap paper he had, Harry wrote to Mick Twomey. He folded it carefully and licked the two-*anna* stamp, slapping it on the envelope addressed to Mr Michael Twomey at the Victorian Football League, Melbourne, Australia. The always optimistic Harry hoped his Australian footballer friend would remember him.

He then watched the postman pass his house every day for the next three weeks. How long does a letter take to reach the land Down Under? Would Mick Twomey reply? Would he even consider sponsoring a penniless young eighteen-year-old boy from India?

Papa Sean came home one evening two and a half weeks later and summoned Harry to sit by his side. He looked serious. Harry wondered what rocket he was up for now. Slowly his father pulled out an envelope from his pocket. It had an Australian postmark on it.

'This came through my international sorting box at the post office this morning, son. It wouldn't have been delivered till tomorrow. Thought you might like to have it earlier.' Papa Sean smiled.

Harry's hands were trembling uncontrollably. He found it difficult to get the envelope flap open.

The letter was short, and Harry read the few lines of the message quickly.

Dear Harry,

I would be proud to sponsor the most unstoppable eighteen-year-old I know.

I will commence the process immediately.

Welcome to the land Down Under.

Yours truly,

Mick Twomey

The letter clinched the application, and when the final official acceptance letter from the High Commission of Australia arrived in the post, Harry almost hugged his mother to death in his exhilaration. His years of hard work and focus on his goal had paid off.

He was going to Australia—to start a new life and to play football.

It was two weeks to the day till Harry's departure to Australia. He kept counting his few rupees, all he had managed to save from his wages. There was not much left to buy a new shirt. The best hand-me-down from his elder brother would have to do, with his black school trousers, which were a bit worse for wear but still held the crease. He didn't own a pair of shoes, but he would ask Jeremy if he would let him have his worn-out suede lace-up oxfords.

Mother Meg and Papa Sean were overjoyed and bursting with pride, but anxious about their third son leaving for a faraway land on his own. They did not have the funds to go to Australia to settle him in, but knew that nothing would change their determined young son's mind now. Harry was the most enterprising of his brothers. He got into scrapes more with his daredevil nature, but always came out on the right side of things. He seemed to be looked after by the Powers That Be. Probably because he was such a kind-hearted lad who lived by the courage of his own convictions.

'Sure you can have these shoes, Harry,' Jeremy said, dusting off the suede oxfords. 'Hey, kid try these on.' He threw Harry a pair of corduroy slacks, a cream shirt, a matching blazer, and a plaid vest. Jeremy was a flight attendant with Air India and had the most enviable wardrobe.

Harry was taken by surprise and lost for words.

'Pick your jaw off the floor and try on the clothes, you dumbo!' Jeremy laughed.

The clothes and shoes fit perfectly. Though Jeremy was older he was of slight build, and the brothers were the same size.

Mother Meg walked in just then and burst into tears. Tears of joy. Her fledgling was leaving the nest. And he looked so grown-up and dapper.

It was ten days before Harry was to leave his hometown and family when his best friend Darryl called in.

'You'll be coming to my eighteenth birthday party on Saturday, cutlet, won't you? I've invited some new skirts in town. Glyce Martin is bringing her bestie and it's going to be a fab jam!'

Damn! Harry had forgotten all about the party. His head had been swirling for the past few weeks getting ready for emigration to Australia.

'God knows when we'll meet again, Cutlet.' Darryl punched him in the stomach.

'Ouch! Yaa, man, of course. I wouldn't miss it for the world. See you Saturday.'

GEORGIA

Georgia was born in India to parents who were well connected and respected in political and social circles. At that time India was confronted by the challenge of becoming an independent nation after two hundred years of British rule. Growing up in a wealthy, Anglo-Indian socialite family in India, Georgia, an only child, often felt quite alone.

Her father was a handsome and debonair Anglo-Indian man with an elegant handlebar moustache that fascinated Georgia. He was a bomber pilot in the Royal Indian Air Force, before becoming an air marshal and Indonesian President Sukarno's right-hand man. Georgia had a special connection with her father, though she knew he would never cross her matriarch of a mother in any decisions in order to keep the peace. He commanded a squadron, but was never game to be in the firing line at home.

Marianne married Jon, the fighter pilot, in 1942. Their only child, Georgia, arrived in 1944.

Her parents, Marianne and Jon Hathaway, moved often, to the far-flung places to which the air force sent her father. Her mother was a charming socialite, a ravishing beauty with bewitching green eyes, flawless skin and luxuriant red hair which cascaded down to her shoulders in waves. Her daughter, Georgia, had inherited her mother's good looks and, even at a young age, one could see that she would be a classic beauty when she grew up.

Not having a sibling to play with, or share thoughts and memories with, can be difficult for a child. A dog named Gruff came into Georgia's life at the tender age of one, and he became her virtual sibling. Gruff provided the love and companionship she craved, and it was like having a relationship with a little brother who followed her everywhere. There was no threat of sibling rivalry, and young Georgia doted on Gruff. This love of a dog was imprinted on her as a child and carried on into adulthood. Dogs became the only ones she could trust, when her parents deserted her.

The culture in India at that time did not favour female children, especially female children who were the first born. Georgia was sent off to boarding school in 1951 when she was seven years old.

In those bygone days, many families anglicised their children's names because they wanted to equip them to live good, dignified lives in the future by getting them the best education possible. Christians with anglicised names were accepted in elite schools in India.

Her parents gave her what they felt was a proper Christian name: Georgia.

Later in life, Georgia hated thinking about the time her life changed when her parents learned they would be leaving India for a posting in Djakarta and sent her to boarding school at the tender age of seven in 1951.

Georgia vividly recalled the scene at the train station even fifty years later, and her eyes would fill with tears, just as they had on that frightening day.

Her mother fussed over Georgia's clothing, adjusting an unfashionably printed red polka-dot dress.

'Stand up straight, girl. Watch your posture,' she admonished, and then pushed her toward the train. 'Now get along.'

'Goodbye, Mum and Dad,' Georgia said in a choked voice.

Her dad simply kissed her on the cheek and muttered gruffly, 'Goodbye, daughter. Do well in your schooling. See you in a year or two.'

A year! Two years! Fright overwhelmed her seven-year-old heart as she bravely held back her tears. Georgia waved at her parents as the train pulled out of the station, watching them grow smaller and smaller on the platform as the train gathered speed, until they finally disappeared completely.

Little did she know she would only be catching brief glimpses of her family during school breaks and holidays for the next decade.

The boarding school, an exclusive convent run by the nuns and priests of the order of St. Melissa, was located in the hills of Nainital, in the Kumaon foothills in India.

Georgia was very lonely. Not only did she miss her home and parents, but she especially missed her beloved dog, Gruff.

Her father gave Georgia the white bull terrier on her first birthday; they had been inseparable ever since.

Like other children born in India during the 1940s and 1950s, Georgia was raised to fear and revere her parents. Gruff became her best friend, the only creature on earth she could tell anything without being judged.

She showered Gruff with all her love and affection. Gruff seemed to know she needed him and never left her side. He, like her, was seven years old when she was sent to boarding school, and her heart ached for the one 'person' she felt loved her, who was non-judgemental.

So Georgia suffered and cried heartbroken tears into her pillow at night, wondering what terrible thing she had done to cause her parents to abandon her.

'Wake up, Georgia,' Sister Bernadine called. 'It's 6:00 am. Time to brush your teeth and wash your face. Mass starts at 6:30 am; don't be late.'

Georgia often wanted to turn over and fall asleep again, but she had learned quickly that disobedience had consequences, including being denied breakfast or being made to stand in the corner for an hour. Discipline was important in boarding school.

Tears in the night were dealt with sensibly when what Georgia yearned for was a hug. 'I feel sick; I just want my mum,' she wept one night.

'Try not to think of her. I know it's difficult, but you have to try,' Sister Bernadine said. 'It's really difficult for your mum and dad when they see you so upset. They want to help you and they hate to hear you like this.'

Georgia coped by taking refuge in books. She became a quiet and shy child, mistrustful of other people.

The 'year or two' her father mentioned on parting stretched out. It was three years before Georgia was scheduled for a visit home.

A letter arrived in the mail just before she was due to leave. The brief message read, 'Gruff has died. Your father and I have decided to get another dog, a bulldog.'

She sat on the steps outside her classroom and, though she shed no tears, she felt as though her heart had shattered into a million pieces. Her ten-year-old heart agonised for her lost friend, knowing Gruff thought she had abandoned him to die of heartbreak.

Now there was no one in Georgia's life. The one 'person' that loved her unconditionally was gone. There was no magic wand to wave to take her pain away. No medicine to cure the ache in her heart. She had to learn to cope. There was nobody to run to. No mother's bosom to bury her head in. No arms to enfold a grieving child.

Love became something she learnt to take out of a box and dust off for the holidays, and then put back and shut away during term-time. That was the lesson learnt, healthy or not.

No one gave her the love she had found in Gruff. This passion for her four-legged companions lasted throughout her life, all learned from the love of a dog.

The years passed and Georgia entered her teens.

'What are you doing, Rani?' she asked her best friend, watching her carefully pinning a sanitary towel with large safety pins onto a tape tied around her waist, inside the large navy bloomers they all had to wear.

'I've got my period,' she replied.

'Period?'

'Don't you know? It's when you bleed every month for a few days and you can have a baby,' Rani said.

'But I don't want to have a baby!' Georgia was astonished.

'Silly, you don't just have a baby.'

Puzzled, she innocently asked, 'What do I do to stop having a baby? Can I stop the bleeding?'

'No, you can't.'

'Then how?' Georgia asked, mystified.

'Ask your mum.'

But she didn't. She was too scared to. What would her mother think of her asking such crazy questions in a letter home?

One day, when Georgia was thirteen years old, the bleeding came.

'Rani, I've got the blood.' She ran to her friend with a worried face, stuffing a handkerchief into her bloomers.

'Here's a pad,' her kind friend said and helped her put it on. 'My mum buys me these special. But you must go to Sister Mary and ask her for sanitary towels.'

Ashamed, she went to the laundry, hesitatingly.

'Yes, child, what is it?' Sister Mary looked at her over her spectacles.

'I … I … I'm bleeding. Rani said—'

'Ah, you have your period. Don't worry, child, here are your sanitary towels.' Sister Mary handed Georgia a folded stack of small white towels, two large safety pins and tape. 'Dirty ones go in the sanitary bin in toilet number one. They will be washed and put back in your locker. The ration is one dozen for the week. Use them carefully.'

The last little white towel was used on the third day, so she washed them at night and hung them on her iron bed rail, against the wall where no one could see them. Though she scrubbed and scrubbed, she couldn't get all the stains out and they still smelt a bit. Rani had disposable ones.

But she didn't tell her mother and she kept washing. Besides, she couldn't trouble her parents about such trivial things when they had important cocktail parties and dinners to attend with the president far away overseas in Djakarta.

And she still worried about a baby growing in her tummy. Wasn't that where they grew? She had seen Rani's mum's swollen belly when she came to visit her daughter. Then Rani told her she went to the hospital to have the baby. On the next visit, she proudly showed Georgia her little sibling, a bouncing baby boy.

How did it come out? How did it get there in the first place? She'd have to find out … somehow … somewhere.

Mandy and Eva sneaked out to see the boys from Beaufort High, the boys' school down the road. They planned it all day, whispering and giggling. When the lights went out, they climbed out the window. Jenny and Mary stuffed their beds with pillows and drew the blankets tight over them, so Sister Bernadine wouldn't notice their absence on her night rounds with her flashlight.

The next morning, they were heroes. The story was told and re-told many times, gathering more embellishments with each telling. They had met the boys in the clearing and eaten chocolate cake and had Coca Colas, and then kissed and cuddled and almost did it. It was so tempting when their hormones ran riot, they said, but they didn't want to have a baby. So they didn't.

Didn't what? Georgia wondered. Everyone else seemed to know. They were all a year or two older than her; maybe she would just know the answer next year.

A few nights later, she decided she would do the same. After all, one became a hero and the centre of attention for being so daring.

And she would say she 'did it!' That would be better than Mandy and Eva, and she would be more popular. Yes, that's what she would do. They teased her about Clark, the tallest boy at the boys' school, who looked at her sometimes and winked. When the girls went to concerts at the boys' school, they had to walk in a straight crocodile in regulated heights. She was always at the tail end because she was so tall.

'You should be boyfriend and girlfriend', they said, 'because you are both tall.'

She didn't particularly like him because he had pimples, but she told Rani she was going to see him that night.

'No, no!' Rani was aghast. 'You'll get expelled if you're caught.'

'I won't be, I promise,' Georgia said. 'Don't worry; just let me out the window and stuff pillows in my bed.'

Once out the window, she had nowhere to go. So she sneaked into the quadrangle and found an empty classroom where she hid for an hour, reading a book by torchlight.

Then she heard footsteps and the lights turned on in the quadrangle. Beams from strong searchlights probed every nook and cranny of the netball court. She cowered under a desk.

'Where is that girl? Thought she was the quiet one. Never can tell with these dark horses,' Sister Bernadine's voice rang out. Georgia peeped out through a crack in the door. Sister looked strange in her long nightgown with no veil. She wore a tight skull cap on her head.

Jitu, the night watchman, had been asleep in his chair when Georgia passed him. The commotion woke him, and he jolted upright. There would be trouble if he was caught napping; he might even lose his job.

When the pandemonium died down, she crept back to the dormitory and snuck into bed.

But Rani had told on her, and in the morning she had to face Mother Superior. All hell broke loose. She was expelled in shame and sent to her grandparents, since her parents were still overseas. She was glad they were, this once. She wouldn't have to face them.

Her father was a powerful man, and a week later she was reinstated. Rani steered clear of her. She now had no friends, and no one wanted to speak to her. Being daring was heroic, but being expelled was a cardinal sin.

Boarding school became even lonelier. And now her parents were probably angrier with her and she would never go home again.

She had a lot to worry about, being concerned that she would get pregnant every time her next period came around.

Her father eventually retired from the air force. He built a beautiful home and settled down with his wife in South India, in the beautiful garden city of Bangalore.

During the next seven years in boarding school Georgia rarely went home. Her parents were either travelling to exotic places or too busy climbing the social ladder. An incessant round of cocktail parties, charity functions and political dinners at the president's palace.

Georgia finally re-joined her family at the age of seventeen, to find parents who were almost strangers and did not feel comfortable having a grown-up daughter suddenly in their midst.

THE MEETING

It was the night after graduation, August 1961; the era of rock'n'roll, the Beatles and Elvis Presley—the 'King'— who was Georgia's idol.

She was seventeen and so excited to be out of boarding school and let off the leash, not having to conform to the routine of rising at 6:00 am to kneel on wooden pews in church every morning at Mass, or to be punished for not knowing her 7x tables and made to stand behind the classroom door while Mrs Tanner whipped her calves with a bamboo cane. The swish and sing of the flexible bamboo was more frightening than the actual stinging of the lashes that followed: ten for not knowing her tables and, if they were not learnt by the next day without a fault, the penalty would be double—twenty lashes.

Running wild in the sixties didn't involve anything more than kissing a boy in Cubbon Park under a tree. But was it frowned upon? No, it was a cardinal sin. A stern police officer arrested her one day for 'indecent behaviour'.

The boy who had kissed her ran away and she was left to face the music alone. The policeman drove her home in the police car to face the wrath of her parents.

'You'll bring embarrassment on this family with your unruly behaviour,' her mother reprimanded, as she hung her head in shame.

She was enrolled at secretarial college and did well, becoming proficient at 80 wpm in shorthand and 120 wpm in typing. When she graduated from college she applied for a few secretarial positions and landed one with an aircraft company. Her boss, Mr Sweeny, was a kind man with a lovely young wife and twin sons. He said she was the most efficient secretary he'd ever had.

She encouraged her best friend, Linda, to apply for a job at the same company. Linda was also letting down her hair, straight out of boarding school. She came from a large, loving family of nine siblings and was always welcomed home for the holidays. She had often invited Georgia to her home, but Georgia's parents hadn't allowed it.

The interview test was a letter dictated by Mr Sweeny, filled with technical words only an aircraft engineer could have spelled right. Georgia wanted Linda to get the job because she would be good company for her during a routine and uneventful day. They could have lunch together and discuss boys and fashions. Georgia sneaked a copy of the letter from the filing cabinet and Linda typed a perfectly spelled draft. Mr Sweeny looked at it quizzically; maybe he suspected, but Linda landed the job.

The national beauty pageant was a big event in Bangalore, with semi-finalists being selected to go to the big city, Bombay, for the finals. Georgia secretly entered and won a place in the semi-finals. Linda was ecstatic, and the two friends planned to travel to Bombay together. It would be the first trip, other than the lonely trips to boarding school, Georgia had ever made on her own.

'No daughter of mine will parade in a beauty pageant,' was the stern reprimand from her mother. 'Short skirts and red lipstick like a prostitute!'

Her mother was extremely annoyed, ripping the consent form for contestants under the age of eighteen to shreds.

Georgia's face fell with bitter disappointment, but she didn't dare retort.

The wages at her typing job were paid monthly; a very modest sum of rupees 375, from which she paid rupees 100 for her board at home.

'You must learn the value of money, girl. Nothing is free in this life.' Obviously, even love had a price.

Georgia grew lonelier and felt a misfit in the family. This led to her decision to leave her hometown and spread her wings in the big city. But she didn't have near enough money to pay for her train ticket or support herself for the interim period while she found work in Bombay.

An idea popped into her head: her mother's jewellery. Surely her mother wouldn't miss a small pair of diamonds—she had so many. If she could sell them, she could get away. Her parents wouldn't miss her or the jewellery, she thought.

With her heart in her mouth, she sneaked up to her parents' bedroom and carefully selected a pair of yellow Asian diamonds from her mother's blue velvet jewellery case.

The Brighton's jewellery store downtown in Commercial Street was very posh. The turbaned doorman saluted and held open the door for her as she entered tentatively, trying to ignore the butterflies in her stomach. She knew she was stealing, but she must get away and make her own life. They didn't want her upsetting their organised life.

'Not worth that much, young lady,' said the jeweller, squinting at the diamonds on the black felt cloth on the counter with his eyeglass.

'How much?' she whispered hoarsely.

'About rupees 30,000.' He looked at her coyly, knowing they were worth three times that much.

'I'll take it,' she replied, looking over her shoulder nervously. Then her heart stood still. Walking through the front door was Marianne Hathaway, under full sail.

The jeweller had rung her mother when he recognised the earrings.

That night she lay in her bed in the depths of despair. As she got up to get a glass of water and an aspirin from the kitchen, she heard her parents' voices drifting out from their slightly ajar bedroom door.

'We'll have to ask her to leave, or she is going to bring terrible disgrace upon this family.' Georgia felt the pain of the words like a knife stabbing her in the heart.

The next day, her mother handed her rupees 5000. 'This will bide you over for a month till you find a job, and here's your train ticket.'

Georgia looked down at the little piece of cardboard in the palm of her hand—a one-way ticket to Bombay.

Georgia was to leave her home, if she could have ever called it her home, in two weeks' time. She was apprehensive about facing the great wide world alone, having been cloistered in boarding school for ten years. But the excitement of freedom overcame any anxiety she had. She was a survivor already at a young age, and her fighting spirit would serve her in good stead.

Bring on the world.

The birthday party for Darryl, Georgia's girlfriend's beau, was in full swing. Elvis' hit of the sixties, 'Can't Help Falling in Love,' played on the gramophone:

Wise men say
only fools rush in
but I can't help
falling love with you.

When Harry arrived at the party dressed in his brother's clothes, he looked around without much interest. His mind was far away—in a foreign land.

'Hey, man, come and meet a couple of the new gals in town,' Darryl greeted him. 'Glad you could make it.'

'Not much point. I'm leaving in a couple of weeks, kiddo.' Harry wasn't enthusiastic at all.

'Oh lighten up and enjoy the night. C'mon, I'll introduce you to Norma.'

Darryl steered him towards a buxom red-haired girl wearing overly tight drainpipe jeans almost bursting at the seams.

As Darryl dragged an unwilling Harry towards the target, Harry's eyes took in the room and landed on a tall, willowy young woman with a cascading mane of jet-black hair. He stopped in his tracks.

'Don't chicken out, dude. Norma's great fun,' admonished his friend.

'How about diverting that way,' said Harry, looking at the willowy brunette who was talking to a bespectacled young Einstein trying to explain to her the theory of relativity.

'That's Georgia, Hazza, upper class society chick—out of our league. She's my girlfriend Glyce's bestie. Just out of convent boarding school, I hear. Probably boring and not much fun. Norma's a really good-time girl. Just what you need to loosen up, bumface!'

'I'd like to meet the brunette. C'mon, let's go that way.'
Harry put his arm around Darryl's neck and did a right turn.

'Girls, get into a circle,' shouted Darryl's big brother. He
seemed to be the organiser of the party. 'Boys, stand back
near the wall.'

The girl got up slowly. She was tall and slender, and her
long tresses swung in a cascade of shimmering blue-black,
catching the light as she moved with a slow almost dance
rhythm, turning heads. He red stilettos clicked on the
wooden floor. Harry stopped in his tracks, mesmerised. She
gave him a half-smile as she passed by, and Harry felt a
shiver go up his spine. What was wrong with him? He hadn't
felt this way about any other girl, and there had been a few
in the past couple of years. Girls from his side of the fence.
She was out of his class, as Darryl said. And he was leaving
the country in a few days anyway.

They were playing the 'Honeymoon Game'. The girls
threw their left shoe into the middle of the floor. When the
whistle blew, the boys picked up a shoe and set off to match
it with its owner. The first boy to succeed went on the
'honeymoon' with the girl. The couple had to follow
instructions from the crowd or there were penalties.

Harry quickly recovered Georgia's red, patent-leather
stiletto from the pile and, kneeling at her feet, slipped it on
her left foot.

Georgia's almond-brown eyes shone with mischief. Her
voluptuous red lips teased.

She leaned towards Harry and whispered in his ear.
'Hmm … How far are you prepared to go?'

Harry's friend, Darryl, shouted, 'Go, man, kiss those
lips!'

Elvis crooned …

Take my hand

take my whole life too
For I can't help
falling in love with you.

Everyone cheered with raucous laughter, egging Harry on as he leaned closer towards those lips, voluptuous and inviting. Suddenly Georgia grabbed a bottle of champagne. She shook the bottle till it fizzed and the cork popped, spurting frothing champagne over Harry's trousers … in the appropriate place. The roar of the crowd was deafening! Harry's friend snapped the picture.

In that brief meeting, Harry knew he had met the girl of his dreams, the only girl for him.

The rest of the fun-filled evening was a blur of gaiety, food, dancing and the party games that the young people played. Harry was on cloud nine. All he could focus on was this vision. The way she moved—she seemed to float on air in a blithesome carefree way. Yet there was something about Georgia. A sense of vulnerability and a hint of sadness in those mesmerising almond-brown eyes. Her laughter was sweet and soft, like the sound of tinkling bells. The bespectacled Einstein had cornered her again, and she looked around for an escape.

Harry grabbed a bottle of Coke and sauntered up to her.

'I'm sure you're hungry. I'm starving. Would you like to check out the dining table? Mrs Costa is a great cook. I've eaten many a meal at Darryl's mum's home.'

'Oh thank you. I am rather peckish.' The vision turned her melting gaze on Harry. 'I'm Georgia,' she said simply.

Harry took her firmly by the elbow and steered her away from Einstein. 'Pleased to meet you—again. Though we've already been on a honeymoon, I think formal introductions are a good idea, don't you? I'm Harry, Darryl's buddy.'

'Glyce, my bestie, dragged me here tonight. She thinks I need to kick up my heels a bit after ten years in boarding school. Sorry for drowning you in champagne', she continued—not looking a bit sorry.

Georgia suddenly gasped, looking at her watch. 'It's nearly midnight. I've got to go!'

'Are you going to turn into a pumpkin?' Harry asked quizzically.

'My parents' rules,' she said.

'I'll walk you back, if you aren't being picked up in a limousine,' Harry joked.

Harry and Georgia walked the quiet streets, heading towards the elite part of Bangalore. The houses were bigger, with well-manicured lawns and rose bushes lining the front fences. The people who lived in them were affluent and highly respected—doctors, lawyers, surgeons and stockbrokers. A far cry from the other side of town where Harry and his family lived in little cottages, neat but small. Tiny gardens or none at all. Most homes opened almost onto the street.

Gardeners, plumbers, posties and truck drivers were his neighbours. Hardworking, honest men that worked long hours to provide for their families. He was proud to be one of them.

The young couple strolled leisurely, talking about everything and nothing. The night air was warm and balmy, with a slight breeze rustling through the jacaranda trees. The moon hid behind a cloud and peeped out now and again as they moved down the winding road, which was deserted except for a stray dog or two. Georgia didn't seem to be in a hurry now, despite her parents' curfew. They each knew their lives were to take separate directions imminently, yet neither felt the need to disclose this information to the other. In the moment, there was a sense of peace in each other's company. A feeling of having known one another for a long time.

When they reached Georgia's front gate, they both seemed reluctant to part.

'I'll see you around,' she said, as she lifted the latch.

'Sure,' he replied.

Both knew it wouldn't happen. Neither was prepared to put it in words.

'Infatuation,' Darryl had said when Harry wouldn't join the gang for another date. 'We're young—the world's our oyster; plenty of fish in the sea.'

Not for Harry. He knew—he just knew, even then—she was the one for him; the only one. He wanted to spend his life taking care of her.

Darryl had given him the photograph he had snapped that day at his birthday party of a young seventeen-year-old Madonna … And oh those lips! He wondered where her life would take her.

Georgia left Bangalore the day after the party.

Harry had tried to find her, with no luck. He bravely called on her parents.

'What would a boy like you have to offer my daughter?' was the greeting at the door. Marianne Hathaway, Georgia's mother, sneered at this boy on her doorstep.

He was the boy from the other side of the tracks.

Mother Meg hugged Harry and just smiled. She believed in fate, and that true love finds it way back—if that was what it was.

Three weeks later in August 1961, Harry Haines, with all of his savings, rupees 500, which amounted to £4.00 Australian, wished his family goodbye and boarded a flight from Bangalore to Melbourne, Australia.

And on the shores of Australia eighteen-year-old Harry landed.

THE BIG CITY

It was the monsoon season in July 1961 when the train pulled into Bombay, a big bustling city. A city ancient yet modern; fabulously rich yet achingly poor.

During the journey of 1427 km, Georgia had nineteen hours and fifty minutes to ponder the events of the last few days. She had packed her dresses, skirts, blouses and underwear into a brown leather suitcase. The underwear consisted of conservative white cotton full-panties, slips and pointy brassieres, and her outfits were pretty, but modest, chosen by her mother. The red patent-leather stilettos were the only new addition, purchased by Georgia herself on an impulse.

She mused over the night at Darryl's birthday party, that silly game, and the boy who found her shoe. There was something about Harry Georgia couldn't get out of her mind. Unlike most boys his age, he had a maturity and a deep understanding of people. He was the kind of person she would like to get to know better, with his rugged looks, nut-brown skin, and that deep cleft in his chin. He had a very slim but strong, athletic physique, probably from his love of boxing. As he had walked her home that night, they had exchanged things about themselves that couples do who have known each other a long time, but they had done so in an hour and a half. This was a boy Georgia would have liked to date again and find out more about—if there had been time.

She wondered if he would remember her and try to find her, only to be told that she had left for the big city. He would probably forget all about the chance meeting, and Darryl would introduce him to some other hot chick, like the world-wise Norma.

Little did she know. Harry could not get Georgia out of his mind.

And Fate has a way of playing a part in people's lives—even many years later.

Georgia found board and lodging with Ethel, a lady kind but very business minded. With the money she could afford to pay for her monthly board, an attic room, bare but clean, was offered. This was to be shared with Diana—a bit of a princess. Georgia paid the first month's board up front, leaving her little for bus and train fare, and lunch.

After just a few interviews she landed a good position at Haussler's, an aircraft manufacturing company. She was appointed executive secretary to the CEO, whom she still had to meet.

It was her first day on the job. What should she wear? After discarding many outfits, Georgia chose an elegant cream-and-black suit and pumps, small gold studs in her earlobes and a spray of Chanel No. 5, courtesy of Princess, who advised her to stand up tall and not hunch over. She tended to do this as she was always self-conscious of her height, being taller than her dancing partners in high school.

Catching the 7:15 am train to work, there was only standing room. The train was packed with commuters and noisy chatter, all on their way to work in the city. She was glad to reach her station and get a breath of fresh air as she strolled across the park to her new office.

A friendly young boy greeted her as she entered the building. 'Hey, first day?' he asked with a smile.

'Yes. Do you work here?'

'Sam Batur at your service—bus boy extraordinaire,' said Sam, clicking his heels with a salute.

'Impressive title. I'm Girl Friday to the CEO.'

Sam's look turned serious and surprised.

'Is he that scary?'

'You'll find out in ten seconds. Here he comes.'

A tall, handsome, debonair young man, about thirty, strode across the quadrangle. He was six feet tall with wavy dark hair and green eyes—oh, those eyes! He smiled at Georgia, holding the door open for her. Sam winked and disappeared down the side entrance.

'First day on the job?' asked the Greek God, with a smile showing dazzling white teeth.

'Y-yes,' stammered Georgia, finding no more words.

'Come along then. You must be my new PA. Hope you can take dictation and type. I'm Atik Rahman. Everyone calls me Tics. Do you have a name?' Tics asked, amused.

'Georgia.'

'Come along then, young Georgia.' He led her to a desk in a small room. 'This is your nook. When you're settled in, I'll see you in my office for dictation.'

The first letter she took was all gobbledygook. Tics looked at it quizzically over his horn-rimmed Armani spectacles and returned it to her corrected—rather, all patiently rewritten in his neat handwriting—with a smile of encouragement. It was not that she couldn't take dictation—

she had passed at the top of her class, 120 wpm—but those damn eyes; so disconcerting. She fell in love at first sight.

From the very first day they left the office within minutes of each other to catch the same train. Tics travelled to her station and they had tea and *pakoras,* a tasty Indian vegetable fritter, in the station restaurant.

Georgia found Tics an easy conversationalist and a good listener. She poured out her heart to him, narrating the story of her lonely childhood, schooling in the convent with the nuns and, after all those years, returning home to a family in which she felt a misfit. He came to understand her like an open book.

For two years they spent every moment together. Tics showed Georgia the sights of Bombay and paid her rent when she ran out of money.

Georgia was filled with trepidation about calling her parents and feeling the brunt of their disapproval. She had arrived in the strange city, feeling bereft and forsaken. At least in boarding school the nuns were kind, and she had her fellow schoolmates for company and food on the table. She often didn't eat lunch because the rupees in her purse needed to be stretched till her next monthly pay packet for train fare.

Not a word, letter or phone call at the boarding house on the black phone since she left Bangalore and her parents' home.

'Phone call!' Ethel would shout when there was a telephone call for one of her boarders. It was usually for Princess, who had a host of admirers calling to take her out to dinner and the movies. Never for Georgia.

'Learn to stand on your own two feet,' Georgia's father would say. She had been left to do that from the age of seven. When other kids had their parents' support and went home for the holidays, she spent many Christmases with the nuns, who tried to make the season happy for a young girl.

Grandpa Andy came up to the boarding school sometimes and they went to the movies and canoeing on the lake. All the treats were paid for by her parents, with generous allowances for her to buy what she pleased. She was always the envy of her girlfriends in school, with her expensive clothes and perfectly pleated skirts. But it was not the same—not the same as going home and spending time with her parents, hugging them or sitting on her father's knee.

Did she ever do that? She couldn't remember ever being spontaneously kissed by her mother or father—only an occasional peck on the cheek—or enveloped in a bear hug. She watched her friends with their families and was envious of the love and easy friendliness they shared. Georgia went home about every two or three years and, in between, spent some holidays with Grandpa and Nana in Poona. She adored Grandpa Andy, and they spent many companionable hours together visiting the zoo, show grounds and park.

'I need money for a haircut,' Grandpa Andy would say to Nana. Money was tight and there was nothing extra for frivolities, as Nana called them. Two *annas* would take them to the zoo and buy ice cream cones in those days. Grandpa was almost bald, but Nana never questioned the haircut. Georgia loved their little secret and giggled delightedly every time.

Georgia felt she didn't have a childhood, but those few precious memories were tucked away to be savoured.

Bombay is 'the city that never sleeps'. In the hours of darkness, lights illuminate, and music reverberates in its streets. With the growing influence of western culture, copious numbers of nightclubs, discotheques and bars had sprung up. To young Georgia this was all exciting but overwhelming. She had led a sheltered life till now, but Tics—quite the man of the world—delighted in teaching her the ropes. They spent many wonderful nights together, dining and dancing the night away.

Tics was an excellent dancer, and Georgia loved dancing, which was the one skill she had learnt at the convent. The nuns were particular about young ladies learning the art of foxtrot and waltz. The girls also spent many hours dancing rock'n'roll to Elvis Presley songs: the jive, twist, mashed potato, hippy-hippy shake and the limbo.

Georgia was quite good at the limbo, and they had great fun entering a dance competition, which she won, taking home a huge life-sized stuffed lion as the prize. They named him Puggy and he travelled in the backseat of the car around Bombay city, causing quite a stir when they stopped to enjoy the tasty local food from the *cartwallahs* down Juhu Beach. This was the famous beach of Bombay that features in Bollywood movies. Many stars chose this place as their abode and the culture had grown, with lavish restaurants and hotels having cropped up.

Here you could savour the appetising local snacks of Bombay: the spicy *bhel puri* and *pani puri*. On weekends it became quite an extravaganza, with toy sellers, horse and donkey rides, dancing monkeys, acrobats and cricket matches.

Georgia and Tics spent many romantic evenings on the beachfront, watching the breathtaking sunsets. He stole her heart, the tender young heart of an eighteen-year-old girl.

One night she lost her virginity—the night of the festival of *Holi*.

Dressed in sandals, a strapped top and long flowing skirt, Georgia walked briskly down the quiet street, headed towards the city to meet Tics. The warm humid evening breeze blew softly through her long black tresses. An auto-rickshaw slowed down alongside, hoping for a fare. Georgia waved him a 'no' signal.

Two sari-clad women with fruit-laden baskets balanced on their heads, hips swaying seductively, passed her by, avidly engrossed in the conversation of the day. Two little girls played hopscotch on the pavement; the game was drawn with chalk on the concrete. They were happy and smiling with the joy of carefree youth.

As she neared the city, she heard the noise of people singing and drums beating. *Holi*, the festival of colours, was in full swing.

As spring warms the landscape, southern India cuts loose for a day of high jinx and general hilarity—a day of spring fever. *Holi* is an exuberant festival where young and old flirt and misbehave in the streets in an uninhibited atmosphere, throwing coloured water and powder over each other.

Mature women form groups and apply colours to each other's foreheads and exchange greetings, kissing one another on both cheeks. Children take special delight in spraying colours on each other, and throw coloured water balloons at passers-by, and young lovers apply colours to their beloved. There is a popular legend behind this. It is said that the mischievous Lord Krishna naughtily applied colour to his beloved Radha to make her love him. The trend soon gained popularity amongst the young-in-love.

Tics was waiting for her at the corner—their favourite meeting spot. He was wearing the traditional white *juba,* now covered in all colours of the rainbow. As Georgia approached, he showered her with blue powder. She was prepared and doused him with green and gold. They chased one another, laughing and throwing clouds of colour, and joined the throng of young lovers dancing in the street. The uninhibited sexual atmosphere of other lovers fanned the flames of their passion and Georgia felt those arms wrap around her in a passionate embrace. They lost themselves in a deep kiss, their young, searing passion consuming them.

That night, Tics took Georgia back to his apartment by the beach. After a shower, with the water running in rainbow colours off their bodies, they lay down together on his divan bed with the balmy sea breeze blowing through the open window, billowing the white mosquito-net canopy around them. To the sound of the waves washing onto the shore, his strong, gentle hands stroked her, his lips travelling down her neck to nestle in her cleavage. She felt a shiver run through her body and a wetness between her legs. Being young and in love was exhilarating, and the way he touched and kissed her simply fanned the flames of their love into a bonfire of passion.

His caresses were new and wonderful. He was confident and experienced, in contrast to her newly found sexual need: gentle, sexy and erotic, all rolled in one. Not frightening. Knowing what he was doing. Her nipples rose as his lips moved across a breast, startling her.

'Shush … it's all right. Just listen to your body,' he whispered huskily, his voice full of desire. As his lips closed over a nipple, tugging on it gently, she was transported to another planet. The first feeling of him entering her was like a warmth that spread through her entire body, and every thrust into her only increased the fire to a level she didn't know she could feel.

He moved slowly, rhythmically, within her till she cried out with ecstasy, arching her hips to meet him. There was a sharp pain—brief—then the spasms of her first orgasm engulfed her body in waves. It was pure bliss.

As she pressed him hard against her that night, Georgia knew that what her schoolmates had whispered about when the lights were out as the nuns did their rounds was nothing compared to what she experienced with Tics, her first true love.

She was a woman now—in the complete sense of the word.

Georgia and Tics spent many romantic evenings dining and dancing and talking into the night, and then making passionate love. She couldn't get enough of him—her Greek God.

FORSAKEN

Georgia loved Bombay and its film industry.

Bombay, the city of dreams, housed the centre of the Hindi film industry—Bollywood, one of the biggest film production centres in the world. Bollywood produced nearly one hundred movies in 1962, with its popular stars Dev Anand, Raj Kapoor and Dilip Kumar being the hot favourites.

Bollywood got its name from the merger of the city's name, Bombay, and Hollywood, the American film industry capital. The movies churned out there were a major source of entertainment to an audience of 469.1 million people.

Georgia loved spending the day in this film city's core—a world where you could not differentiate fake from real, as things were so perfect. Dotted with fountains, gardens, lakes, helipads and real-looking buildings, the film city was sprawled over a large expanse. The well-appointed indoor and outdoor shooting facilities, editing and recording rooms, ranked this studio amongst the best in the world.

As Tics and Georgia wandered hand in hand and she excitedly pointed out the superstar on set, Raj Kapoor, her hero, Tics told her of his dreams to be an actor. Yes, she could see him here, starring in his own movie; she would be his leading lady. He was red-hot; the starlets would swoon. She wouldn't have a chance of keeping him to herself.

Fortunately, he was the CEO at Haussler's and wasn't disappearing to stardom. A comforting thought.

'I'm going to Hollywood.'

'Hollywood in America? How could you do this to me?' said a stunned Georgia.

He said he loved her but would never be able to marry out of his caste, which was Brahmin Hindu. He didn't want to hurt her. His mother was an orthodox woman and would not allow the marriage to a Christian under any circumstances. She was terminally ill, and if he went against her wishes, it would kill her. He cared too deeply about his mother to take that risk. It would be better if they parted ways.

Then he was gone. Gone as if he was never there. Gone forever. Leaving her heart-broken—the tender heart of a first love.

Georgia would have followed her beloved Tics to the end of the earth and supported him throughout his acting career. She couldn't understand why he wouldn't spread his wings in Bollywood. But no, he said—it was Hollywood he'd always dreamed about.

He did not love her, or want her. No one did. Not her parents and now not the man she had given her heart to.

She cried alone and didn't eat for weeks. Princess understood to a certain extent, but simply told her, 'He wasn't worth it; you'll find someone better,' as she preened her hair and gave Georgia a big hug.

Never mind. She was strong and brave and had always been able to face life. No matter how the cards were dealt.

Until now.

It was late Autumn 1968 in the hill country of Gosford, New South Wales, on the beautiful central coast of Australia. Large deciduous trees, including oaks, elms, poplars, and Japanese maples exploding with colour painted the landscape in shades of crimson, orange and bright yellow foliage. Harry Haines watched the fading sun sink lower from the wraparound veranda of his parents' farm-style home set in the picturesque Hunter Valley, which boasted a tranquil ambience and clean fresh air. The signpost read 'Meg & Sean Haines' Lookout Farm Welcomes You.' The house, named Silver Oaks, located on ten acres on the slopes of rolling hills in Pokolbin, was charming.

The day they moved in, Mother Meg paraphrased a Ralph Waldo Emerson quote, saying, 'When I bought the farm I did not know what a bargain I had in blue-tongued lizards, parrots and cockatoos, kangaroos and bush turkeys—as little did I know what sublime mornings and sunsets I was buying.'

It was rundown and unkempt, but years later they had, all three, worked hard to turn it into one of the most popular family lookout farms in the locality. Harry loved the land and gardening, and had a passion for all creatures great and small.

It was seven years since Harry had landed on the shores of Australia. Mick Twomey had taken the young Harry under his wing and treated him as his own son. When Harry had completed his Bachelor of Commerce degree, he landed a position working for the Australian Secret Intelligence

Service. It was a top-secret job, which took him to the capital city of Australia, Canberra.

Mother Meg and Papa Sean fulfilled their dream of a better life, migrating from India, sponsored by their only unmarried child, to the land Down Under.

'You would make someone a good husband, son,' Mother Meg sighed.

Harry had dated other girls in Australia over the years, but hadn't met anyone who remotely interested him. It was his own fault, he knew. His heart had been taken prisoner and sometimes, as he drifted off to sleep, he wondered if he was destined to be alone forever. Would his heart give up carrying the torch for a seventeen-year-old girl?

Harry spent many weekends on his parents' property in the Hunter. It was only a few hours' drive from cold Canberra. He loved to come down here, where the climate was temperate all year round, and sit on the porch with Jib, the old sheep dog.

Jib had been hit by a car as a puppy, and his owners left him at the vet to be put down. Mother Meg was in the veterinary clinic that day with Jane, the Alpaca, when she met Jib. He came home with her, and was a healthy and happy dog, grateful to have found a family that loved him dearly and where he was free to roam on the property with the other animals. Visitors, particularly the children, loved him, and Jib enjoyed all the pats and attention.

Here Harry found peace. He had learnt the art of meditation from an old friend, a Buddhist. 'Let the mind be still, empty,' Hunza said.

But today Harry's mind wandered … back to a party seven years ago; the night he met Georgia. She would be nearing twenty-five now. Did she ever think of him? Her face never left his mind. It appeared in every leaf, every flower, every pond and stream; it haunted his dreams at night. Where was she now? Married, probably, 'to someone of her own status'.

Harry was three months from his twenty-sixth birthday; not too old, but old enough to be lonely. There was something that kept a distance between him and any woman who started to get close, something he wasn't sure he could change even if he tried.

The evening passed, remaining warm and balmy. Harry half dozed to the sounds of nature, the birds, wildlife and forest sounds of the Australian bushland. A baby kangaroo came up to the porch looking for food. Jib raised his head but did not move. A bush turkey busily scratched away in the underbrush, building its nest.

Harry's mind drifted back to a warm night such as this, seven years ago, and playing that silly game. His friends pushed him into it, and he found himself on the sofa next to Georgia, while Elvis Presley belted out songs on the record player. Closer and closer to those lips, he daydreamed—feeling a stirring in his loins—

'Hi, son!' Papa Sean's loud foghorn voice jolted him upright. 'We're back. See you've stacked the hay and done a mighty good job with the fence, m'lad.'

Mother Meg dropped a kiss on his head as she lugged a bagful of shopping inside. 'Wash up. It's your favourite tonight, rack of lamb and a mess of vegetables.'

After dinner Harry sat on the veranda again, this time with Papa Sean, Jib at his feet. The dog never left Harry's side when he was there.

'You can't wait all your life for a woman who doesn't even know you exist, my boy.'

Sean had a soft spot for his third son. Though parents are not supposed to have favourites, he shared a special bond with Harry. There was no doubt Harry was his favourite child. He just wished Harry would find someone to share his life with. He worried that his son was such a loner.

'Jenny called, by the way, Harry. You should ask her out. Nice lass. Make some lucky man a good wife.'

Harry liked Jenny. She was good company, but, damn it … He was just not interested in that way and didn't want to give her the wrong idea.

That night, Harry Haines knelt down at the side of his bed and poured his heart out. 'Give me a sign,' he prayed.

THE DISMISSAL

Georgia was happy. In fact, she was on top of the world. It was 1968, a glorious autumn day in Canberra, the capital city of Australia.

With the exodus of Anglo-Indians out of India in the droves, her parents Marianne and Jon Hathaway decided to leave in a hurry.

'Phone call, Georgia,' Ethel had yelled out from below the stairs one afternoon. Georgia was not sure she had heard right as she jumped up from her bed in the attic room.

'Me, Ethel?' she asked hesitatingly from the top of the stairs.

'A man, Georgie!'

Surely it couldn't be …

'Georgia, I'm calling to tell you we are leaving for Australia. I have put you on our application. I suggest you migrate with us. India will not be a suitable place for our kind any longer.' Her father's voice was curt on the phoneline. She hadn't heard from her parents in over two years. Did they really care? Since Tics had abandoned her, she had not dated anyone else, though Princess had been kind and offered to take her on a double date with her beau's friend. Oh well, she might as well see what opportunities this new country would bring. She didn't have anything to lose. Georgia had boarded the plane with her parents and arrived in Canberra, Australia, two years ago.

The autumn leaves formed a carpet of shades of brown and gold, crunching under her feet, as she swung her beauty case, almost skipping down the road to the college. She loved her job as head beauty teacher at Belle Femme and couldn't wait to see her students in class that day. The bright morning sky, the noise of traffic and young mums pushing prams, framed an attractive, elegant twenty-five-year-old woman as she walked up the front steps of the college. Georgia entered the foyer and hung up her coat in the staff room to reveal the chic college uniform with a logo embroidered on the right pocket. She waved and blew a kiss to bespectacled Pat, the receptionist, and smiled at a couple of students on their way out.

One of the best-loved and most efficient teachers, she walked down the corridor to her classroom. She was a whole hour early today. It was a lesson on body wrapping, requiring a lot of set-up in advance. She was very organised and keen to get started.

Georgia pushed open the door to her classroom, the Orchid Room. Muffled sounds. The room was dark, blinds drawn. Reaching for the light switch, she stopped, surprise registering on her face as she heard:

'Ugh—oooh—give it to me—you're the best—' *Thud thud thud.*

'Bitch!'

'Yeah, I like it when you talk dirty, Ivan.'

Ivan? Georgia was aghast. *Not Ivan my boss.* He was

married. Recently married. The scene became clearer as her eyes adjusted to the dim light in the room, and the whole picture came into focus—a man and woman on a massage couch, going for it. Just as she was about to leave silently in shock, Ivan looked up. His eyes meet Georgia's on his final thrust.

'AHHH!'

'Was that good?' a panting woman's voice asked.

Georgia beat a hasty retreat.

Georgia's class was well underway, with five students lying on massage couches, while the others worked on them, painting mud and seaweed body masks and wrapping them in cheesecloth.

'Georgia, can you have a look at Esther's skin?' asked seventeen-year-old Janie. 'She's come out in a red rash.'

'Wash it off immediately, Jane. Did you ask if she was allergic to fish, shellfish and such?'

Jane looked sheepish and replied hesitantly, 'No …'

'I break out when I eat prawns,' piped young Esther.

'The seaweed wrap isn't the right one for this client, Janie. Next time check all the contraindications first. Into the shower, Esther, immediately.'

Georgia is a bit out of sorts, thought Esther.

'Something's upset our good-natured teacher today,' whispered Esther to Jane. 'I wonder what. Let's hit the showers.'

Just as the girls were about to make a beeline for the washroom, there was a knock on the door.

'Ivan's come to perve,' giggled Jane with a mischievous

look.

Pat, the receptionist, stuck her head around the half-open door. Her large, horn-rimmed spectacles always seemed to precede her face into a room. She was all spectacles and big blue eyes as large as saucers.

'Georgia, the boss would like to see you in his office after class.' Pat's voice carried a question mark that you could almost hear. She was quite surprised that Ivan had asked her to summon the number-one and most popular teacher in the college in a very stern voice that spelled trouble. She'd heard that tone of voice when she'd been asked to fetch a student for reprimanding, but Georgia? She was curious and very worried. Like all the other staff and students at the college, she adored their best-loved head teacher.

'OK thanks, Pat.' Georgia raised her eyebrows and her heart thudded in her chest. *What am I in for?*

The students stopped working, listening in curiously as Pat replied, making a face, 'Doesn't seem to be in the best mood—good luck, Gigi!'

Students quickly resumed their tasks as Georgia turned around. Dead silence.

'Hope you're not going to get fired,' burst out eighteen-year-old Samantha unceremoniously.

Jean, mum of three, frowned. 'Shut up, Sam. Get on with the wrap. I'm freezing!'

Georgia walked amongst the workstations, adjusting a wrap, mixing a mud mask, and helping a student apply the product. Pensive and worried. *What now?* What could she ever say to her boss about what she had seen?

Apprehensively, Georgia knocked softly on the large oakwood door which was slightly ajar. The gold embossed lettering on the door read: Ivan Grant, CEO.

'Enter!' boomed a man's voice.

Ivan sat writing at a large desk with a leather top and black desk lamp. Clearly a man's room. Beauty magazines were scattered on the coffee table. There was a comfy beige sofa with a red throw and black and grey cushions with arty sketches of women's faces and bodies.

'Come in. Close the door.' He did not look up from his writing.

Georgia entered. Shut the door gently. Waited.

Ivan swivelled around in his chair, lowering his Armani spectacles.

'We'll both forget this afternoon. It didn't happen.'

Georgia looked him in the eye but didn't respond. He walked up to her, arms folded. Georgia held her ground. Ivan moved closer and ran his finger down her left cheek.

'You value your job here, don't you? You're a darn good teacher. Students love you. That makes you an asset.'

Ivan's smarmy face was so close now she could smell the garlic and onion on his breath, probably from the greasy burger he'd had for lunch. A wave of nausea almost overcame her. He traced his finger across her chin and up her right cheek.

'Real beauty too … It could be a profitable partnership. Let's say I start with a generous bonus in your pay packet. As I said, today didn't happen.'

Georgia gave him a scathing look, turned on her heels and headed for the door.

'You're FIRED!' Ivan shouted.

Hesitating for just a second mid-stride, Georgia strutted out, her head held high, red stilettos strumming an angry beat on the parquet floor.

FATE

Mid-afternoon, Canberra dropped to a cold forty-one degrees Fahrenheit. Harry donned his overcoat and tucked in a scarf—the warm goats-hair one Mother Meg had knitted for his last birthday, with the fleece courtesy of Jane.

She had 'de-haired' the fleece, removing the coarse, straight guard hairs to use just the soft undercoat. Harry's mum had then carefully and painstakingly washed, dried and fluffed the fleece before carding the hair with a hand carder and spinning it with a light tension. Harry stroked it with love for a mother who was the most wonderful, caring, hardworking person in the world. Every cent was saved, and now she and Papa had a winning business they loved and justly deserved.

Harry's one weakness was comics, and a detour past Zany's comic shop in Canberra was on the agenda today.

About to enter the quirky comic shop on the trendiest, classiest and most elegant shopping street in the city, Harry did a double-take and thought, 'Is this another figment of the imagination?'

A young woman slammed out the front doors of the beauty college, Belle Femme, a couple of doors down. She seemed upset. Red stilettos clicked hurriedly down the steps, missed a step and she went tumbling, books flying out of her arms and becoming airborne, before coming to rest on the pavement, pages scattering.

It couldn't be her, Harry thought incredulously!

He took the photo out of his wallet and studied it. Was his mind playing tricks? That was India, and this was Canberra, Australia. What would she be doing here?

Gathering his wits, he rushed to help. As he gathered books and smoothed the pages, the girl looked up. Those lips … it *was* her. Her face had haunted his dreams all this time. How could he forget it? Older, but more sophisticated and so self-assured. Did she remember him? She didn't seem to.

'Impressive,' he commented, hoping she couldn't hear his heart thundering in his chest so loudly. It felt as if it was going to jump out and land on the sidewalk. 'You did that like a pro!' Then, as she brushed away a tear, his eyes turned to concern. 'Sorry, are you hurt?'

'Just a broken heel.' She examined her red patent leather stiletto shoe.

The shoe.

She looked at him curiously. Those big brown eyes sparkled with mischief and those lips formed a pout.

'You don't remember me, then?'

Harry was taken aback. It was such an impossible question. She did remember him. That was a good start.

'I thought my mind was playing tricks. It couldn't be you here, across the other side of the world. What a coincidence!'

Or was it?

'Give me a sign,' he had asked.

Mother Meg always said, 'Nothing happens by coincidence. Everything is to plan. That is the order of the Universe.'

'We moved here a couple of years ago. What're you doing in this neck of the woods?' she asked, looking up at him with those melting brown eyes.

'I migrated seven years ago, completed my Bachelor of Commerce degree, and landed a position with ASIS in Canberra.'

Her eyes twinkled mischievously. 'How could I forget someone I almost went on a honeymoon with? Too late for compensation? Buy you lunch? I'm starving.'

'Let's get that shoe fixed first.' Harry smiled as he helped her up and gathered the rest of the books, his mind still in a whirl.

The afternoon was surreal. As they lunched together in a European-style cafe, the years seemed to slip away. They had never really known each other, yet he felt he knew her like no other. She had lived in his memory and in his dreams. Had she ever thought of him since that night? She had never tried to contact him, but her parents would not have allowed it. Was that the reason? Did she ever want to find him?

'Let's go to the record store after lunch,' her voice interrupted his thoughts. 'I want to see if that new Elvis album is out.'

So she was still an Elvis fan.

At the Towers Record Store, Georgia put on headphones and her feet tapped to 'Blue Suede Shoes.' Harry played Chopin's 'Prelude in E-Minor', orchestrating as it played.

'Surely not!' She made a face at him.

The quirky comic store was next. Old Max greeted Harry with a surprised smile and said, 'First time I've seen a lady with you interested in comics then, m'lad.'

'Tweety and Sylvester—my favourites,' she replied. That lilting voice was music to Harry's ears.

'Not a Superman fan, eh?'

'There aren't any supermen in my world. I like the strong quiet type,' she replied teasingly. They left with two copies of Tweety and six of Superman.

'Do you actually read all those?' was Georgia's surprised question.

'I'm the quiet one that turns up in the red cape to rescue damsels in distress. Didn't you know?' Harry quipped awkwardly.

They spent the afternoon strolling through the trendy malls and looking in antique and memorabilia shops in London Court. Georgia fell in love with an antique pendant of a cute cocker spaniel with sad blue sapphire eyes. Harry purchased it for her and fastened it around her neck.

She pecked him on the cheek. Those lips … so close. Some people smile with their lips, but she smiled with her eyes—those big, brown, smouldering pools of molten lava. Harry could have drowned in them.

'Thanks, Harry. You didn't have to do that,' she protested.

'You didn't get a honeymoon present after all. Now we're square.'

As Georgia turned to admire the pendant in the store mirror, the shop doorbell tinkled, and a well-dressed middle-aged woman entered.

Not Mum's best friend! Georgia thought, as she looked in the mirror. She was the last person she wanted to meet now and have to introduce Harry to. Andrea Forthright was the town crier, and the word would be back to her mother within the hour and published around Canberra from north to south within forty-eight hours.

'Hullo, Georgia,' Mrs Forthright's voice rang out, giving Georgia no choice but to turn around and force a smile.

'Good afternoon, Mrs Forthright,' she replied tentatively.

'I have a message for you from Lauren. Was going to drop it off at Marianne's. I'm having coffee with her this afternoon,' Mrs Forthright said, handing her the note. She looked at the pendant around Georgia's neck. 'What an exquisite antique pendant,' she said.

'He looks so sad,' commented the young store assistant. 'Glad he's found a good home. May I help you, Mrs Forthright?'

As Mrs Forthright turned to the showcase, pointing out some earrings she'd like to look at, Georgia glanced at the note, disappointment registering on her face. Screwing it up, she aimed it at the waste paper basket and turned back to the mirror, fingering the pendant pensively. The paper ball missed its target and landed at Harry's feet. As he picked it up to deposit it in the waste basket, a few words jumped out at him: 'sorry … can't … have a great birthday tomorrow.'

The day ended with the movie *Romeo and Juliet*. As the credits rolled—THE END—Georgia wiped her eyes with her lace handkerchief. None of the girls Harry knew, the few he had taken out to the movies, were ever moved at anything on the screen and none would have owned a lace handkerchief. She was a lady, refined and sensitive.

They strolled side by side in a comfortable silence. It seemed they had known each other for a long time. Was it only a few hours ago that they had met? Certainly not for Harry; she had always been there—all the time, all those years. Seven years seemed like only a moment ago.

'Am I forgiven?' He was startled out of his reverie to find Georgia looking up at him with an impertinent smile.

'It was a pretty serious crime. Let's see—a trip to the country with me tomorrow to even the odds?'

'Hm … since I've missed out on seven years of honeymoon …' she teased.

'Where were you?'

'In Bombay. I left for the big city the day after the party,' she replied with a hint of sadness.

Harry looked at her but didn't comment. She would open up more when she got to know him better—or so he hoped.

God, she was ravishingly stunning. Luxuriant raven-black hair gleaming in the afternoon sun hung down to her shoulders and curled gently at the ends. She had matured from a pretty teenager to a self-assured and sophisticated woman, yet there was something lost and sad about her. Her eyes, deep pools of golden brown, seemed to hold painful memories.

'Wear walking shoes,' Harry said brusquely.

Georgia nodded in assent and waved goodbye. Harry saluted, clicking his heels, much to her amusement.

The afternoon was warm and balmy as they drove out of Canberra on the Hume Highway heading for the Southern Highlands. It was unusual for that time of year.

As they passed the historic town of Goulburn, Elvis' mesmerising voice drifted out over the radio, crooning, 'A Boy Like Me. A Girl Like You.' When Elvis reached the end of the song, wishing for a girl who would 'last a lifetime through', Harry sneaked a peak at Georgia out of the corner of his eye and realised it was not a pipedream. She was here in his car with her luxurious black tresses blowing in the breeze with the car top down. Would she 'last a lifetime through?'

As the 1960 Ford Falcon Sprint Convertible II zoomed down the Hume Highway at 70 mph, he knew his heart's desire had come true that sunny autumn day.

The townships of Eaglehawk, Fitzroy Falls, Kangaroo Valley, Bundanoon, Moss Vale and Bowral flashed by as the miles melted away.

Harry pulled over and parked near a charming little coffee house in the picturesque town of Berrima. Tables and chairs were set out under bright umbrellas, and families and couples enjoyed the warm afternoon sunshine.

Georgia, who had been quiet for most of the drive, buried deep in her thoughts, occasionally singing along with Elvis, looked at Harry enquiringly. 'Where are we going?'

'Time for a cup of tea and stretch. They make the best Devonshire teas and have scones and homemade strawberry jam to die for.'

'How much farther?'

'Tired?'

'Not at all.' Georgia smiled. 'I could drive on all day long. I love motoring, especially when chauffeured by a handsome driver.'

'Glad I fit the bill.' He held the door open for her.

'And gallant as well.' She grinned.

Over steaming cups of tea and the most delicious crumbly scones she had ever tasted, with homemade strawberry jam and clotted cream, Georgia looked at Harry enquiringly. 'A hint?'

'Then it won't be a birthday surprise!'

'You know?' Georgia's golden eyes opened wide.

'A little bird told me,' Harry replied with a boyish grin. 'If you could have anything today, what would you wish for?'

Georgia looked thoughtful as her hand went to her pendant.

'If I found him, I'd give him a home,' she said, caressing the cocker spaniel pendant. 'Dogs love us unconditionally, unlike parents.' Her voice drifted off sadly.

'Yours live in Canberra?' asked Harry.

'Don't see much of them. Though I live at home, they're always travelling. Mum has a busy social calendar.'

'You'll like my mum.'

Surprised, Georgia looked at him questioningly. 'Am I going to meet her today?'

'Yes.'

The scenery changed as they drove into the beautiful Hunter Valley with its luscious vineyards flanking the road on both sides. The car turned into a dirt road which led up a curving driveway through breathtaking liquid-amber sunlight, maple trees and ponds to a farmhouse at the end. Lookout Farm's welcoming sign made Georgia smile: 'Love is a fruit in season at all times, and within reach of every hand.'

'How charming!' she exclaimed. An old border collie bounded up to the car, barking excitedly.

'Hey, Jib, old guy!' Harry patted the dog, who slobbered all over him in return. The farmhouse door burst open and a buxom, grey-haired woman, wiping her hands on her apron, emerged excitedly.

'Hi, Mum,' Harry said as he enfolded her in a bear hug. The warm connection between the pair was clear to see as Harry drew Georgia by the hand and introduced her to his mother.

'Good afternoon, ma'am,' Georgia said, smiling shyly at this kindly, loving, motherly person, whom she warmed to instantly.

She had always been a good judge of character. Either she took to someone straightaway or she felt uneasy.

'Happy birthday,' was the smiling response.

'Does the whole world know?' She jostled Harry.

'Busy little bird.'

As they sat around the enormous, homey farmhouse table, laden with a delicious lunch, Georgia could feel the warmth in this family, a warmth she never experienced in her parents' home. Meals in her parents' home were very formal occasions without much conversation except for polite small talk. She was always afraid to say the wrong thing and be criticised or judged.

'Here's to your good health and happiness, young lady,' Papa Sean's booming voice interrupted her thoughts.

Harry's gaze was on Georgia; he couldn't believe that this girl that had lived in his memory for seven years was right there ... right beside him. Mother Meg looked at her son and smiled knowingly.

After dinner, Georgia helped Mother Meg clean up in the kitchen. Harry's mum was so comfortable to be with, so unintimidating. The young woman, longing to be mothered, and the homely, buxom woman, arms up to the elbows in suds in the kitchen sink, wispy strands of hair blowing around her kindly face, seemed to form an instant connection.

Mother Meg was so unlike her own mother, who was always immaculately groomed, aloof and unapproachable.

'I'm sure Harry would like to show you his birds.'

'His birds?' Georgia looked surprised.

Mother Meg was amused. 'The feathered kind—homing pigeons. His pride and joy.'

Harry poked his head around the door. 'Ready for that walk?'

Drying her hands, Georgia looked enquiringly at Mother Meg. 'Run along. I'll finish up in here and make Papa his cup of tea.'

They walked through the U-pick gardens, where people picked fruit: young couples in love, families with children, and the elderly with their walking sticks. It was the season for apples—Batlow, Pink Lady and Granny Smith—and stone fruit—peaches, nectarines and plums. Harry picked a large peach and handed it to Georgia. She bit into it, juice running down her chin.

'Mm …'

Those lips. Harry leaned in. Georgia looked into his eyes. They kissed gently. 'That's for the honeymoon,' she whispered teasingly with a glint in her eye.

'Yeah, thanks. I've been hanging out. Race you to the hay stack!'

Harry sprinted off, Georgia a close second. She was fast and nimble and soon caught up with him, falling face first into the hay.

As she dusted herself off, hay sticking out of her hair, Harry looked at her appraisingly and teased, 'Great hairdo. You should leave it.'

She punched him, taking off to the next point of interest: The Busy Bee Learning Centre. They watched the bees make honey.

'I'd like to be a queen bee; all those males at my feet.'

'Madam Queen Bee, I'm at your service.' Harry bowed with a flourish. 'Your chariot awaits.'

He led her to the little station where young and old were awaiting the small, scenic train which took visitors on a ride around the twenty-five acre property. They sat up the front next to old Jack, the train driver.

'Jack, this is Georgia; city girl.'

'Mighty damn pretty lass, m'boy!'

Georgia blushed as Harry turned around and announced to all, 'It's her birthday!'

She had never felt so happy and acknowledged in her own family as she did with these wonderful people, who accepted her so unequivocally. She remembered all those birthdays in boarding school she faced alone. Large parcels arrived filled with chocolates, her favourite books, designer clothes and shoes. Everything a young girl could fancy. She gave most of them away to her schoolmates, who eyed them enviously. Her heart ached for the warmth of family and the simple pleasures of life—such as she experienced this wonderful day, her twenty-fifth birthday, in the warm sunny Hunter Valley at Meg & Sean Haines' Lookout Farm.

'Last stop! All out!' Jack's booming voice snapped her out of her reverie.

'OK?' Harry looked at her anxiously.

'I'm starving,' she announced.

'Know just the thing.' He led her to the play area and a hot dog stand. Ordering two hot dogs with sauce, mustard, cheese and onions, he handed one to her. They sat on a cosy picnic bench watching the kids having a whale of a time.

The petting zoo was crowded, with children amongst the emus, donkeys, goats, rabbits and sheep. Georgia got close up with a miniature donkey and an inquisitive emu.

They raced each other through the burlap maze, getting lost and cooeeing to find each other. At the last stop Harry blindfolded Georgia. 'Don't peek.'

'Hint, hint!' she demanded impatiently.

A birthday party was laid out in the farmhouse, cake, gelato and everything a kid at heart could want. The whole group from the train was gathered around.

'Surprise!'

Harry whipped off the blindfold with a flourish. They all clapped.

Wonderment filled her face as it dawned on her that this was all in her honour. All the birthdays of a lost childhood rolled into one. Happy tears filled her eyes.

On the drive back home, Georgia was quiet and thoughtful. 'I would have loved to see the pigeons.'

'That's for another day; something more important awaits.'

'There's more? What? What?'

'Patience, woman,' he replied sternly.

As they drove up to a farmhouse, old John, hobbling with a cane, came up to greet them. He walked with a limp, having been fitted with an artificial limb since he lost a leg in the war. Didn't stop him. He ran the local dog boarding and breeding kennels and had for over twenty years.

'They're in the barn,' he waved, pointing to the right side of the house.

A litter of cocker spaniel pups, four gold females and one black male, about eight weeks old, tumbled playfully around their mother, a blue roan, mostly black with a distinctive white streak on her forehead and a white tip on her black, bushy tail.

'Oh, they're adorable!' Georgia exclaimed.

'There's one born to be your son,' Harry said softly.

The black one waddled up to her like a little duck. He was just like his mum, with the white markings; just adorable. Georgia picked him up gently and looked into his bright sapphire-blue eyes that looked so sad. She touched her pendant.

'He has a fault,' John said. 'No one wants him for a show dog. You could have him for half price. My son named him Truman, but you could change his name.'

The puppy licked a salty tear trickling down Georgia's face as she held him close and felt the beating of his little heart.

Driving back to Canberra, the pup was snuggled in his basket, a tiny bundle of joy, happy to be adopted.

Georgia looked out the window silently, deep in thought.

'Is a penny enough for those thoughts?' She was startled by Harry's voice.

'Not worth it. I like the name, Truman … my son,' she whispered dewy-eyed. 'Thanks for a wonderful day and the best birthday present ever.'

'Hey, can't have a birthday without a party and a pressie.'

Georgia glanced at Harry, almost uncomfortable with the unprecedented amount of attention showered on her that day.

Harry wondered whether he was awake or dreaming.

EXIT

Georgia sneaked in the front door, putting the basket with the little pup down in the hallway. He was still fast asleep; like babies, young puppies need a lot of sleep.

As she hung up her jacket on the front hall stand, her mother's sharp voice made her jump.

'Is that you, Georgia? You're late.'

She never felt comfortable with her mother and always walked on eggshells around her. Marianne Hathaway, elegant and aloof, had hard features; one could not imagine her bearing and nurturing children—they would be too much trouble.

Georgia felt she was banished to boarding school at such a young age because she was in the way.

Had time softened Marianne Hathaway's motherly instinct, Georgia wondered. Did she regret sending her only child away at that tender age?

'Where on earth have you been?' Annoyance crossed her mother's face as Georgia entered the drawing room where she was seated on the sofa, with a glass of wine in her hand. 'Your father and I have been waiting on dinner—it *is* your birthday, after all. Happy birthday. Your present's on the table.'

Georgia went up to kiss her, but she turned her cheek away and the kiss just brushed her face.

'You are a mess, child. Leon will be here in a minute. Go and get washed up,' her mother said, frowning as she looked at Georgia's muddy boots. 'His family are pillars of society and well-heeled; he'll make good husband material.'

Georgia knew better than to retort—besides, Truman might wake any moment. She nodded and dashed off.

Dressing to sit down to a stiff, formal dinner with her parents and Leon—pompous Leon, with his smarmy face and know-it-all looks—was the last thing she wanted to do on her birthday.

Harry, on the other hand, was so strong and kind, with a warmth that made you feel comfortable. He was not bad looking either, with his rugged face, sinewy arms, athletic body and muscularity, which stirred something deep inside her. She hadn't felt that way since Tics. Georgia wondered where Tics was now. She hadn't heard from him at all. He was probably climbing the ladder to success in Tinsel Town, with a dozen starlets chasing him.

She was older and wiser now; no man was going to leave her like that again. She wouldn't have it; no, next time she would be in control … if there was a next time.

Harry was a nice guy, but did he care for her in that way? Maybe he already had a girlfriend he was committed to. Georgia wondered if he had thought about her at all over the years since they met at Darryl's birthday party. It seemed such a long time ago. She had fleetingly thought about him now and again, but her mother would have blown a gasket had she mentioned him.

'A boy from the other side of the tracks,' Marianne Hathaway would have sniffed disapprovingly.

She wondered if he really liked her now.

Now fate had brought them together again and it had been a wonderful day, a birthday filled with happiness and fun. Harry had invited her to dinner as well, but she had reluctantly declined, not wanting to bring down her mother's wrath on her head. She knew they didn't really care if she was home or not; it was probably too much trouble to worry about her birthday.

She fleetingly wondered what was in her presents. They were exquisitely wrapped, as on all the birthdays before. Her mother would have the store assistants wrap all those designer cardigans, skirts and blouses—it would be too much bother to wrap them herself.

There was never a card, only the gifts immaculately bowed and matched with the gift-wrapping—so impersonal, so cold. She bet Mother Meg wouldn't give store-bought gifts; she'd make them—like Harry's angora wool jumper.

'Ah, well,' she sighed, picking up little Tru, who had stirred and started to inspect his new quarters. 'Better get ready for dinner.'

She chose a simple white dress with a V neckline and a single strand of pearls. They complemented her olive skin, and her glistening black tresses made a startling contrast against the white of the dress. Small pearl drops in her earlobes and strappy gold sandals completed the outfit. Glancing at herself in the full-length mirror, she drew a hairbrush through her long hair once more and blew a kiss to Tru.

'Now be good, little man. I won't be long.'

She placed her stuffed frog and kangaroo in his basket to keep him company, along with a small ticking clock. She had read that puppies feel comforted by the sound of the ticking—they think it's the beating of a heart.

A loud knock, and her father poked his head around the door. 'Can I come in, pumpkin?'

Jon sat on the edge of the bed and put his arm around his daughter. He had a fondness for Georgia and thought his wife was too hard on her, having sent her away in disgrace at the age of seventeen. However, he was not prepared to overrule the matriarch and generally went about his work, playing golf and clubbing in a quiet, unobtrusive manner, leaving her to run the house and family.

'Now, what have we got here?' He smiled, petting the puppy. 'Don't think your mother's going to be pleased.'

Georgia rested her head on her father's shoulder. 'He's my son, Daddy. Harry gave me Tru for my birthday.'

Jon's hand brushed his daughter's luxuriant black tresses off her face. She was stubborn and independent. She had grown into an attractive young lady with a timeless, classic beauty—the kind men leave their wives and give up everything for; the woman men die for.

Leon was certainly not the type for her, whether his father was a shipping magnate or not, Jon thought. But he was not prepared to cross Marianne and incur her wrath; he had to live with her.

'Harry?' he asked.

'He's the kindest person in the whole world, Daddy. You'll like him.'

'Let's get ready for dinner. Happy birthday, girl.'

Dinner, as usual, was a grand, formal affair, laid out with her mother's fine English bone china, silverware and Waterford crystal, and served by the maid in her starched apron. It was a far cry from the farmhouse table with its blue-and-yellow checked tablecloth and thick white plates—so warm, welcoming. And the food! Oh so delish.

A yapping came from the bedroom.

'Is that a dog?' Marianne exclaimed incredulously.

'His name is Truman; *my* dog, Mother.'

'No dogs in this house! I absolutely forbid it. He's to be out by the morning.'

'But—'

'That-is-final.'

Georgia looked pleadingly at her father, but he averted his gaze and did not respond. Throwing her napkin down on the table angrily, she replied quietly, 'We'll both be gone tomorrow,' as she stormed out.

THE PROPOSAL

One year later ...

Georgia and Harry were in the pigeon loft while Truman chased butterflies.

The loft had an indoor as well as an outdoor area. The outdoor area was caged in with wire, so the pigeons couldn't fly away and were protected from predators, such as possums, hawks and the neighbour's cat.

Inside were roosts for the pigeons to sleep on high off the ground, as well as small tubs used as bathing pans, and self-waterers for the pigeons' drinking water. Straw, hay and pine needles formed nesting material for the pigeons to lay their eggs in. Male and female pigeons mate for life, and once they decide to breed, they work together in building their nests.

Georgia had grown quite fond of Harry's pigeons and loved to spend her free afternoons down at his parents' farm, watching Harry train his pet birds.

In the year since she had left her parents' house with Truman, she had never been happier. Harry's parents asked no questions, but simply accepted her.

Georgia's father was a kindly man with a handlebar moustache that Georgia loved to twirl as a little girl. Jon, a fighter-bomber in World War II, commanding a squadron, would never cross his domineering wife. She kept him well under her thumb. However, Jon had a soft spot for his daughter.

A week after her tumultuous departure she received a letter from the bank requesting her to come in on Friday at 3:00 pm.

Sitting upright opposite Mr Mathew, the bank manager, she nervously twiddled her thumbs in her lap. Was her account overdrawn? Since she had lost her position at Belle Femme, her bank account had been dwindling, but she thought she still had enough not to be in the red.

Mr Mathew handed her an embossed white envelope. She recognised with surprise her father's air force squadron crest and scrawl on the envelope addressed to her.

Unfolding the matching headed notepaper, a sign of affluence, with his name and crest in the right-hand corner, Georgia was puzzled.

The short note read: *Georgie, I have deposited this money to your account. It is part of my retirement benefits from the air force. Keep this between us. Good luck. Father*

Mr Mathew handed her the deposit slip with the comment, 'Lucky girl!'

Georgia found an enchanting, quaint little cottage, just on the outskirts of Canberra, in the township of Bungendore, near the internationally acclaimed Bungendore Wood Works Gallery.

'Carpenters Cottage' belonged to old Mr Gong Browne. Gong was born in Holland in 1894 and spent his early working life as a carpenter in the cottage building industry. In 1935 he purchased a stone-fruit orchard and, while waiting for the trees to mature and give him an income, he grew tomatoes and took up woodturning to supplement his earnings. As Gong became more deeply involved in woodturning, it started to dominate his life more and more and, in 1947, he sold his orchard and took up woodturning full time.

When Georgia leased the cottage in 1969, Gong was seventy-five, and woodturning was still his passion. He was constantly developing new techniques, designs and ideas, which he readily shared through his popular demonstrations, teaching sessions and seminars, both locally and overseas.

Gong had an acute awareness that the wood, and the trees it comes from, as well as the talent and ability to craft fine pieces, were God given.

Since his wife of fifty years died the previous year, he could not bear to live in the cottage. Every corner brought back haunting memories of his beloved Martha.

Childless, Gong Browne moved into the room at the back of the gallery when his wife passed away. It was sparse but comfortable. He had lost the zest for life, but always stopped to pat Tru and seemed to like dogs, though he had never owned one.

Recently restored, the cottage was tastefully and comfortably furnished with a vintage charm. The 1930s cottage had white clapboard siding, green shutters and sweet gardens which evoked a simple past and restful living. The original maple floors had been polished and all modern amenities installed.

Georgia was lucky to see the cottage advertised on the first day, in the *Canberra Times*. Gong was happy to find someone to lease the cottage, so like his dear wife, he said; and Georgia promised to look after it for him, as if it was her own.

Truman loved the bubbling brook running across the back of the property and the grassy backyard with its oak trees and rabbits and lizards to chase. Georgia liked living out of the city in the peace and tranquillity of this little village. It was only a thirty-minute drive into the beauty college in Canberra in the morning.

Her own beauty college: Georgia's Art of Beauty Training College.

With the generous sum of money her father had left her, Georgia had taken the plunge and found premises in Dundas Court, Phillip, in the south of Canberra.

'No excuse now not to set up your own college,' Harry had encouraged. Together they found the unit on the ground floor of the building, which did not need much alteration. The sign went up the front, and the pink-and-white striped awnings, already in place, matched perfectly. The twelve training couches, which Georgia had designed with Gong's help, were made of solid Tasmanian oak wood with thick cream-coloured padded upholstery, stitched with a breathing hole for massage and slide out table for cosmetics. A slatted shelf below was to hold the neatly rolled up towels. Gong worked on the couches day and night, and they were transported to the college by Harry and Gong in his truck. They looked neat and professional, lined up in two precision rows, six on each side of the training room.

The beauty equipment, magnifying lamps, creams, nail polishes, make-up, waxes, tints and loads of towels, sheets and other products were delivered each day. Georgia spent many hours late into the night setting up her business, with Truman inspecting everything with his inquisitive nose.

When the first advertisement went out in the Yellow Pages and the *Canberra Times*, Georgia was swamped with applications. A news reporter arrived at the doorstep and took photos, much to Georgia's amazement and pleasant surprise. Her college featured on the front page of the *Canberra Times* that Sunday. The twenty-four students she needed for the first year of training filled the enrolments.

Georgia was in business for herself.

The autumn weather was turning cold, dropping to forty-one degrees Fahrenheit in early May. Tru walked with her along the winding path to the village store in the evening to collect the milk and bread, enjoying the falling leaves of every shade of brown and gold—rolling around in them, delighting in the crunch and fresh smell of the strewn leaves.

They were rugged up well with the red beanie and scarf Mother Meg had knitted her and the red wool jumper for Tru. Her mother had never made her anything in her life.

What were her parents doing now, she wondered. She hadn't seen them at all since that night on her birthday. They were away travelling when she went to collect her things, and Sally the maid said they wouldn't be back till the spring. Did they miss her?

Except for the letter her father had left her at the bank with the money, not a word, telephone call or a letter in the past year.

Matilda fluttered noisily and settled on Georgia's lap as she was let out of her pen, and Percy strutted around, proudly preening his feathers.

'Hey, Percy and Mattie, looks like you've tied the knot,' Harry murmured to the birds. 'Your home's finished. You've been busy. Time to feather the nest, Mattie. Look after her, Percy. She's yours to care for now.'

Georgia watched Harry as he opened the pen of six young birds he was teaching to fly. They flew around crazily, some hitting the ground. She wondered what it would be like to be taken care of, to be loved by a man like Harry. He was so strong, so capable and so solid. A girl would feel safe with him, cared for; he was the kind that would mate for life, like Percy and Matilda.

The new birds found their wings and took to the air as Harry pulled out an old fob watch from his pocket.

'One hour. Let's see if you're ready for the big take-off,' he said, as he set the timer.

Harry cleaned the bathing tubs and filled fresh water and food containers. A small brush-tailed possum jumped out of the oak tree onto his shoulder.

'Oh! Hello, Spike.' Georgia laughed, startled.

Harry scratched the little animal's head, with its pointed snout, pink nose, long whiskers and large ears affectionately.

'Looks like you've had yourself a feast for breakfast up the acorn tree.' He smiled. Spike darted off after more breakfast.

Harry finished up the cleaning chores and joined Georgia on the blanket on the grass. Percy sat on Harry's shoulder, and Mattie hadn't left Georgia's lap, cooeeing and cleaning her feathers.

'When they fly away together, what'll happen if one gets lost? Will they find each other again?' Georgia asked pensively.

'They're well trained to come home. Sometimes they may get captured or injured and can't fly, but as long as they're alive, they'll try to find one another and come home, even after many years.'

Harry looked at Georgia with sadness and longing. He loved her deeply, but hadn't much to offer her. What would she want with a boy from the other side of the tracks?

'Will you find me, Harry, if I get lost? Will you still be here when I come back?'

He looked at her with shyness, avoiding her eyes. 'You can always count on me, pigeon. Spread your wings and fly; have a safe journey.' Choked with unspoken words, he launched Percy and Matilda on their homing flight.

Georgia and Harry stood side by side, watching the birds fly beyond the horizon. What would their journey bring to Percy and Matilda … as well as to Harry and Georgia?

Georgia reached for Harry's hand as she turned and looked at him with her melting brown eyes. He almost drowned in them.

'Marry me, Harry.'

Harry felt he was a heartbeat away from Heaven.

THE WEDDING

It was a simple wedding.

The hall at the Haines farm was decorated with streamers set out across the entire ceiling and cascading down the walls. Hung high over the front door was a large horseshoe made of plywood, painted in blue and silver, which held confetti. This masterpiece, made by Harry, had a trapdoor that had to be operated by a string to allow confetti to shower on the happy couple. Much planning and many trials were done to get it working just right.

'The horseshoe is a symbol of luck. The arms of the horseshoe need to face upwards so that the luck collects in the bowl of the horseshoe,' Harry instructed his brother, Alf.

'Your luck has already come in, bro, marrying the most beautiful girl on the block,' Alf retorted enviously.

'Yeah, and what's left for us?' Conrad chimed in, anchoring a bunch of streamers into the centre of the ceiling and hoisting the horseshoe up as Harry and Alf manoeuvred the arms into place.

'Hey, watch your step,' hollered Conrad.

Too late. Alf toppled off the ladder and the whole contraption collapsed, just as Mother Meg and Georgia walked through the door to see what the boys were up to. Harry and Alf collapsed on the floor with laughter, and all three boys rolled around as confetti spewed out of the horseshoe, covering everyone.

Mother Meg shook her finger at them, dusting confetti off her head. Georgia fell on the floor laughing with the boys.

'Still some luck left,' chided Alf, peering into the hollow of the horseshoe.

'Clean up this mess, you boys.' Mother Meg dusted more confetti out of her hair. 'So much to do; no time for these shenanigans,' she said sternly, but with a twinkle in her eye. She couldn't be happier that her son had found the girl of his dreams after all these years.

Yes, she thought, smiling, *dreams do come true.*

She already loved Georgia as her own daughter and longed to nurture this lovely girl, to mother her like a child and give her back some of her lost childhood. They had formed a bond instantly the day her son had brought her to the farmhouse, and the friendship had only grown stronger over the last year. After five sons, Georgia filled that space in her heart for the daughter she'd never had.

Georgia adored Mother Meg and felt she fitted into a family at last. Papa Sean and Mother Meg were so loving and non-judgemental; never critical, they accepted people for what they were and always saw the good in them.

'If you love someone, you love them for what they are and do not criticise them for what they're not,' she'd said in one of those heart-to-heart talks Georgia had grown to love.

The morning of the wedding was bright and sunny, delivering the kind of weather any bride would want on her special day. Harry, Alf and Conrad were in an old Chevy travelling to the church.

Suddenly the Chevy swerved away from a cow meandering on the busy road, narrowly missed other passers-by and crashed into the back of a truck loaded with apples and chickens for the market. Apples spilled onto the road and chickens ran away, causing chaos with the other traffic

Drivers honked and swore at them, shaking their fists angrily. The Chevy blew a gasket and spewed smoke as the truck driver jumped out of his truck, swearing with a vengeance.

'Crazy man! I'm calling the cops!' he yelled at them, commencing to call in on his car radio.

'Hey, my bro's gettin' married! Get us to St. Patrick's church, dude. The bridegroom's gotta arrive before the bride!'

'Aha.' A slow grin dissolved the angry look on the young driver's face. 'Martin Schumacher, at your service. OK, hop in.'

Honking and driving recklessly, he weaved in and out of the traffic.

'This is riding in style.' Alf grinned as they slapped each other on the back, giving high-fives gleefully.

At the front of the church, guests were milling around. Mother Meg, who was panicking at her son's late appearance, caught sight of the truck as it approached the church door. Horror crossed her face.

Dusting off Harry's jacket as he alighted from the truck, she scolded him. 'What's this, young man? I'll have a word with you later! Get into the church. The bride is about to arrive. Thank God she's late. She may change her mind if she sees your mad antics.'

The boys entered the church, bowing to the guests, who were highly amused by the whole show. Harry and his best man, Alf, took their places at the altar where the priest waited with the two bridesmaids. Conrad disappeared up the stairs to the choir. He was an exceptionally talented organ player, having won a scholarship to the prestigious Royal College of Music in London. He would be leaving in the autumn.

The bride failed to arrive.

Eighty-two-year-old Father Josef looked at his watch, fanning himself.

It was thirty-two degrees Celsius inside, and even with the ceiling fans going and the windows open, he was hot in his ceremonial robes.

'Let's go outside for a breath of fresh air till we see the bride's car approaching,' he announced. Everyone moved outdoors.

Melissa and Liz, the bridesmaids, teased Harry.

'May have to find another bride in a hurry,' quipped Melissa, fluffing her hair.

'Georgia's folks … Don't see them. Maybe they've kidnapped her,' retorted Liz.

'Shut up, Liz.' Melissa gave her a dark look.

Father Josef thought Harry was flirting with the girls and glared at him disapprovingly.

'Here she comes,' yelled Alf as the bride's car approached.

The congregation re-entered the church hurriedly.

Georgia stepped out, looking a vision in lace and satin, and took the arm of Papa Sean, who smiled at her reassuringly.

'If you must marry that boy,' Marianne Hathaway had sniffed, 'we won't be at the wedding.' And they weren't.

Jon Hathaway would have liked to have been there. Georgia was so much like him, strong-minded and independent. He thought Harry was a fine young man with his head on his shoulders, but again … he had to live with his wife.

To the strains of 'Procession of Joy' by Hal Hopson, Georgia walked proudly up the aisle on Papa Sean's arm, as Mother Meg wiped away tears.

It was a shame Georgia's parents weren't there, but Mother Meg loved this girl with all her heart and vowed to make up for all the pomposity of her upper-class family—supposedly so right, so keeping up appearances, so toffy-nosed … so cold.

Father Josef was cross with all the delays and carry-ons. He just wanted to sit down to his cup of tea, blueberry muffin and afternoon siesta—an every-afternoon, three o'clock ritual he looked forward to.

Looking over his glasses he muttered to himself, 'Surely, they have the wrong man in position. Not the one flirting with the bridesmaids. He can't be the one getting married.' Father Josef grabbed Alf's arm and put him in Harry's place, commencing the ceremony.

Mother Meg, agitated, rushed up to the altar and whispered to the priest, putting Harry back in his place.

Father Josef looked shocked and wagged his finger at the naughty bridegroom.

The ceremony proceeded without mishap until the exchange of rings, when Nelson, the five-year-old pageboy, who was now totally distracted, dropped the cushion carrying the rings and they rolled off the cushion down amongst the aisles.

The guests sitting in the front pews scurried to retrieve them. The best man offered two rings off his key chain.

Father Josef, whose sight was fading fast, accepted them and proceeded with the marriage blessings. Mother Meg, feeling faint, fanned herself as Papa Sean smiled and winked at Harry, who turned around just then to see what all the kafuffle was about.

Harry looked at the girl at his side, now his wife—all he had ever dreamed of.

And so they were married. Key rings and all.

EARLY MARRIED LIFE

Carpenter's Cottage seemed the natural place for the young couple to live during the first years of their marriage. Harry moved his few bachelor possessions— clothes, a bike and his treasured Ford Falcon—to the cottage.

Truman was ecstatic to have his new housemate and seemed to know he had acquired a dad. Harry took the dog for long walks through the fields and down by the stream, played endless ball games with him and, in the evening, they all sat by the log fire as the autumn days turned into winter and the evenings grew chilly.

A couple of months after the wedding, the phone rang one evening, startling Tru out of his nap. Georgia grabbed it expectantly, looking at the clock: nearly 6:00 pm. It must be Harry on his way home from work. He always called to let her know he was on the bus home.

'Halloo,' she sang.

'Hope you're happy in the slums with that pigeon boy,' Marianne Hathaway's voice rang sharply in her ear. Georgia still felt like a five-year-old child being reprimanded when her mother spoke to her.

'And how are you, Mum?' Georgia replied, annoyed that Marianne's incessant nagging could still intimidate her. 'My husband's an assistant director at the department, Mother. I love Harry.'

'Love flies out the window soon enough, when the dollars and cents run out and that man keeps you barefoot and pregnant,' Marianne snapped. 'We've given you all the best in life, just to see you to come to this. Now, if you'd married Leon—'

'Goodbye, Mum.' Georgia slammed down the phone, and then sat down abruptly, feeling the tears well up in her eyes and trickle down her cheeks. She was still hurt her parents did not attend her wedding, but that was the story of her life; nothing she did was ever good enough for them.

Even when she came first in class in boarding school and Sister Bernadette gave her a gold star, and she excitedly told her mother on the rare occasions that she rang, 'Well done, child,' was all she said. 'It's important to get a good education.'

Once or twice she came second in class just by losing a mark in maths and once even third. She'd always tried her very best, but sometimes Marcie beat her. Marcie didn't mean to, she just did. And Marcie's mother was always happy with her marks and praised her for trying her best no matter where she ranked in class. But Georgia was terrified at what her parents would say when they got her report card.

One dark evening she left the bolts on her classroom door slightly undone when it was her turn to lock up. That night after prayers, she crept downstairs and shook the bolts till they dropped, and then eased quietly into the classroom. The teacher's exercise book was in her desk up on the dais. Carefully rubbing out the numbers, she changed them by a couple of points, bringing her up the notches to first place. She hoped Mrs Higgins, who was a bit short-sighted, wouldn't notice the rubbed-out figures. She didn't.

The next day when she called out the places in class— 'Georgia, first in class again'—Georgia sighed with relief.

Her parents wouldn't be angry. She had cheated—but they wouldn't know, and they would still love her.

Truman jumped onto her lap and Georgia stroked his long silky ears, burying her face in the dog's fur. He made small sounds of love, telling her he would always love her.

Always.

Just because she was his mum.

Angry and frustrated, Georgia grabbed her coat and walked out into the late evening sunset, tears still blinding her. With her head down she didn't notice Harry coming up the street until she ran into him.

'Hey, beautiful lady, can I buy you a drink?' Harry smiled as he caught her in his arms.

'I don't accept favours from strangers,' she retorted grumpily.

Harry looked surprised at her glum face. He reached out and put his arm around her. 'Aw, c'mon, just this once. Guaranteed to make you smile as well.'

He broke into cartwheels and finished off with a flourish on his knees at her feet as passers-by smiled in amusement. Georgia couldn't help laughing in spite of herself.

'I make an exception for crazy strangers,' she replied, linking her arm in his as they headed off down the road to O'Leary's, the local pub, for a beer.

Sipping her drink, Georgia looked glum-faced. 'Wish we could swap mothers.'

'She call today?' asked Harry gently.

'Thinks I should have married that pompous Leon.'

'Hey, you're looking at the new Director of the Department of Infrastructure,' Harry said, puffing out his chest.

'Serious?' Georgia looked at him, her glum expression changing to excitement.

'Appointed this afternoon. Mr Kelly is retiring next week.'

Georgia sprang up, hugging Harry, spilling his beer

As they entered the cottage a little later, Truman bounded up to Georgia. As usual, he only had eyes for her.

But this time Georgia turned to Harry, passionately kissing him and jumping up to entwine her legs around his waist. Harry was taken by surprise. She was usually not so uninhibited, but he liked it.

Harry carried her to the beautiful canopied bed. The classic, romantic four-poster bed that graced the cottage bedroom had belonged to Martha's grandmother.

As he stripped off his tie and jacket, she shed her top and skirt, panting with unbridled passion. God, she was so beautiful and sexy, Harry thought. She didn't know her own power; any man would be putty in her hands.

Tonight she was insatiable, taking the lead in their lovemaking. He had never seen her this way. Not that he was complaining. He loved his tigress like this; she had a body that would drive any man wild.

Spent, they lay side by side as Elvis Presley came on the radio to join them for another memorable occasion, crooning, 'I'm Yours.'

My love I offer you now,
My heart and all it can give,
For just as long as I live, I'm yours …

As the song ended, Harry sang along softly, 'Now and forever, sweetheart, I'm yours.'

Georgia was his everything. Tonight, Harry felt maybe she could love him half as much as he loved her … But it didn't matter: he loved her enough for both of them.

As the seventies rolled in, Paul McCartney and his group the 'Fab Four' released their final album *Let it Be* before the group broke up. Indira Gandhi, the only woman to hold the office of the prime minister of India, won a second term in a landslide victory.

Harry, Georgia and Truman settle into a comfortable family life. Mother Meg and Papa Sean were a great part of their life and everything she longed for as parents. Sometimes Harry wondered whether she'd married him only to be part of that.

'I married you just because of your mum and dad,' she once teased him.

He was glad she fitted in with his family and they loved her in return. It certainly wasn't the case with hers; they hadn't seen or heard from Georgia's parents since the phone call months earlier that upset his wife. Harry wished he could change it all, but, as his mother wisely said, 'Everything is healed in its own time, when one is ready. Georgia has you to look after her now. I only hope she doesn't break your heart, my son.'

'Mum, why on earth would you say a thing like that?' he asked, a bit annoyed. But Mother Meg just hugged him and ruffled his hair.

Though things were almost always peaceful at the farm, there were exceptions. One such visit started out quietly, to celebrate Papa's birthday, and Mother Meg was cooking up a storm.

Georgia and Harry were playing with Spike, while Percy and Matilda were in the field near the pens. It was the racing season, and Harry was racing his pigeons against some of the best homers in the Hunter Valley Pigeon Club. They would drive further out of the valley this afternoon to launch Percy and Matilda on their journey, one of the longest they had flown.

Papa Sean was up the oak tree trimming branches.

Suddenly, they were all startled by a loud yell— 'Shiiiit!'—and Papa Sean landed in the thorn bush, sending the pigeons fluttering and Truman berserk.

Papa Sean spent an hour face down on the bed, his trousers around his knees, as Mother Meg painted his backside with oil and removed the thorns one by one with tweezers, a painful process. At every 'ouch' there was a peal of laughter from his wife and son.

Truman spun around, dancing doughnuts as Georgia poured boiling water into the teapot and put the lid on.

'Tea's ready when you are,' she called out. 'Truman, it's not something to dance about,' she admonished, secretly smiling.

Tru paid no heed, yapping his head off, spinning faster.

THE BEAUTY COLLEGE

The beauty college was doing well and the business growing. Georgia was a good business woman. Her secretary Lauren—a twenty-six-year-old feisty Italian girl—had become her right hand and a good friend.

It was mid-December 1972, and all the enrolments at the college for the year ahead had been filled before the Christmas holidays. here was always a waiting list to get into the college to study the Diploma of Beauty Therapy as a career. Georgia had commenced the interviews and chosen her twenty-four full-time students for the year. There were twelve girls in their late teens, seven young mums, four women in their thirties and forties who were looking for new careers, and a seventy-two-year-old who wanted to learn the ropes to open a salon with her three daughters already in the field of massage and beauty.

One applicant, Eileen, couldn't understand why she didn't get accepted into the beauty college. She was beautiful and so very keen. But Georgia didn't choose her students on their looks alone. Young girls thought a beauty career would be fun and games, putting on make-up and preening themselves. Quite the contrary. It was a career dedicating oneself to working hard to help others gain confidence and self-esteem by good grooming, skin care and personal hygiene, as well as providing services to relieve stress, fatigue and muscular aches and pains with massage and spa therapies. She taught her students that 'beauty was from within' and everyone benefitted from beauty treatments, not just the rich and famous.

Jane and Jessica, sisters who had been accepted into the college, had rung that morning.

'Dad has suddenly been transferred to Melbourne, so we have to withdraw. Bummer,' Jane said.

Georgia refunded their deposit and wished them well, giving them a referral to a good beauty college in Melbourne.

Should she call Eileen? She had seemed very keen; in fact, desperately so.

Eileen had rung Georgia when she received the standard letter in the mail: 'Sorry, your application to study at the college was not successful this time. We wish you well.'

'What's wrong with me?' Eileen wanted to know. 'I need to have this piece of paper.' Why did she need this particular piece of paper? Georgia would call her to come in for a second interview and find out.

As she picked up the phone to call Eileen, a loud motorbike pulled up at the front of the college. Parking his Harley Davidson, a burly, bearded young man put his helmet on the seat and sauntered through the front reception door to be greeted by Lauren, who looked at him curiously.

'Can I help you?' Lauren asked.

'Want to apply for study here,' he replied.

'This is a beauty college,' Lauren answered. 'The technical college is next door.'

'Come to the right place,' he insisted. 'Diploma of Beauty is what I want to study.'

Georgia, listening in to the conversation, was intrigued. She did need two more students. Buzzing Lauren's office, she spoke into the intercom: 'Send the gentleman in.'

'Are you sure?'

'Yes, Lauren.'

Henry sat opposite the principal of the beauty college looking earnest.

'So you want to study the career of beauty therapy, young man?'

'Yes, ma'am. Set up my own practice, a unisex salon in Sydney, when I'm qualified.'

'I see.'

'I've saved up for the course as well as establishing the business, ma'am. Just completed a certificate in business management as well. Came top of the class.'

He laid a folder of qualifications and references on her desk. Georgia read through the file. She was impressed with his confidence. It seemed this young man knew what he wanted and had taken action. She admired that in people. 'A gentle giant, a warm and caring person of high intelligence,' read a reference from his last teacher. 'Will go far in life. Henry knows what he wants and works towards his goals. He is focussed and persistent.'

Closing the folder and handing it back to him, Georgia looked at Henry over her Dior spectacles.

'You're in. But there will be a couple of rules since you will be in a class with twenty-three females. Does this bother you?'

'No, ma'am,' he replied.

'See Lauren on the way out to fill out your enrolment forms and pay your deposit.'

'I have all the money to pay up front, ma'am.'

Surprised, Georgia replied, 'As you wish.'

'Thank you, ma'am.' Henry was so excited. Today was his lucky day. Georgia wondered whether it was hers. She wasn't usually so hasty in making a decision, but there was something about Henry and she was a good judge of character.

'Students call me Georgia, Henry. Happy to have you on board.'

Picking up the phone, she called Eileen.

Eileen couldn't believe her ears when she heard Georgia's voice on the phone. 'I can be at the college within the hour,' she said.

Impeccably dressed, every hair in place, Eileen was visibly trying to contain herself. 'Thanks for giving me a second chance.'

'Why do you need to study this career?' Georgia asked.

After a slight hesitation, Eileen replied calmly, 'So I can give up my other job, which makes me a lot of money.'

'Don't you like it?'

'Not particularly, but since my husband died recently, I didn't have the skills to do anything else. I have four children to support.'

'I'm sorry.' Georgia was concerned. Eileen didn't volunteer any more information and she didn't like to press her. She could see Eileen hadn't come to terms with her husband's death. It must be difficult to cope alone with four kids at her young age. Georgia's heart went out to her.

'I have all the money, Mrs Haines, to pay up front,' Eileen said. 'You don't need to worry that I can't pay my fees.'

Another surprise. It seemed to be the day for surprises.

'Okay, Eileen. See Lauren on the way out to complete your paperwork. Monday morning 9:00 am sharp. See you in class.'

The year promised to be interesting and eventful.

At the end of the day, Lauren poked her head around the door and brought in two cups of coffee. 'I'm exhausted. Going to soak in a hot bath and put a masque on my face. How about you?'

'A decision to make first.'

Georgia looked at Lauren hesitantly. Lauren detected a fleck of fear in Georgia's eyes. 'Can I help?'

'No, thanks. Just hope I make the right one.'

'OK. See you in the morning.' Lauren looked at her boss with concern.

Georgia never was very communicative about her feelings. All Lauren knew about her was that she did not get on very well with her parents and passionately loved dogs. But she was an astute businesswoman, and the college and salon were growing rapidly into a flourishing business. Students came up from the coastal towns, and the salon was exceedingly popular in Canberra.

Though the capital of Australia, Canberra was small enough for everyone to know everyone else. If you had a good reputation, 'word of mouth' was the only advertisement you needed. A bad one and you'd have to leave town. The college had a particularly good reputation because Georgia was a fair and honest woman who treated everyone as a VIP, from eighty-year-old 'Waltzing Matilda', who waltzed in dance competitions, to little Trudy, the paraplegic who came to the spa for her therapy and massages. Lauren had grown to love her boss and liked her job. The students were a handful sometimes, but filled a place in Georgia's heart. She taught them well, preparing them for their chosen career, but also got too involved, Lauren thought, in their personal lives and dramas—from boyfriends to drugs.

Georgia finished off correcting that last test paper and picked up the phone to call Harry.

'Hi, don't wait up. I'm gonna be quite late. Must finish some stuff tonight. Kiss Tru goodnight for me and don't forget to give him his lamb shank.'

'Miss you,' Harry said, a bit disappointed. He had been looking forward to a quiet dinner and a glass of wine with his wife and Tru this evening. But she got busier as the business grew. Though he was proud of her, he missed the times they spent together in the evening, which were becoming less and less as evening classes were added to the college schedule. Georgia taught most of those herself.

She was driven to achieve. It was an obsession with her, probably stemming back to her childhood when she felt her parents would disapprove if she lost that first place in class.

It was midnight and Harry and Tru had dozed off by the fading embers of the fireplace. Rain was bucketing down outside, drumming on the roof.

A car's headlights penetrated through the blackness and the car screeched to a stop in front of the house. Georgia flew out of the car, leaving the car door open, and ran through the picket gate, which banged loudly behind her. She ran up the path and pounded on the front door in a frenzy. Her eyes were wild, hair streaming and wet in the wind. Her expensive designer silk night shirt, which was all she wore, clung to her lithe, sexy figure, showing the outline of erect nipples. Her feet were bare, with bright-red well-manicured toenails, which matched the bloodstains spattered across her shirt.

She was disorientated and shivering with the cold.

A light went on in the porch as Harry, rubbing the sleep from his eyes, opened the door. His eyes changed to surprise, and then alarm.

'Georgia! What on earth? You'll catch your death,' he said as he grabbed a rug off the back of the sofa and wrapped it around her as she stood in the middle of the living room dripping water. She stared straight ahead with a bland expression.

'I've killed him. I've killed our baby,' she moaned.

Georgia's mind replayed the scene in the doctor's surgery. She was about to have an abortion.

Lying on the surgical couch, her feet in stirrups, the female doctor approached with a scalpel … nearer … nearer…

She screamed!

Harry gently lifted the wet, soggy nightshirt over Georgia's head, as if undressing a child, and wrapped a blanket around her and led her to the sofa. Propping her up comfortably with pillows and tucking the blanket closely around her, he poked the fire and threw another log on before returning to sit by her side.

'I can't be a mother. I'm no good. I wouldn't be able to love any child. I'm sorry, Harry. Thought it would be for the best.' Georgia sobbed uncontrollably.

'Shush. You're the world's best mum.' Harry rocked his wife gently. Truman crept into her lap; he agreed.

She was a lost child herself.

But his baby, his first child … Was it a boy? The son he longed for?

'There is time,' he said softly, as he held her close. Truman licked the silent tears rolling down her cheeks as he laid his head in her lap.

As Georgia drifted in and out of a fitful sleep, she felt a soothing hand on her forehead. 'Rest, my girl. You must take care of yourself.'

'Do you hate me, Ma?' Georgia whispered.

'You have a lot of love to give, Georgia. Every time we decide not to get back at somebody who hurts us, we exercise one of our greatest powers—the power to choose a better way. There'll be more children when you're ready. Sleep now. Love, not time, heals all wounds.'

Mother Meg stroked her brow.

At the local gym, Georgia and two girlfriends worked out on exercise bikes. Mandy was quite a large girl, and Jo, slim and athletic, was four months pregnant.

'Rushed out to pick up the kids yesterday … had a long skirt on … forgot my knickers … thought what the heck, I'm late, not going back,' Mandy gasped as she pedalled the bike. 'Guess what? Tripped, landed on my knees … thought, what's that billowing up round my face … then felt the cool air on my backside—'

Mandy made a face and Jo roared with laughter, just imagining the sight. Jo adjusted her tachometer, speeding up the pedalling.

'Seriously, Jim was talking to our neighbour last night. He told her I had employed the mid-wife to look after him whilst I had the baby in hospital,' Jo said. '"What a good idea!" he said.'

Jo and Mandy broke into peals of laughter. Georgia tried to smile, but tears welled up in her eyes and slowly trickled down her cheeks.

Fortunately, they were too engrossed in their chatter to notice.

SCULLY

Truman sat on the front step of Carpenter's Cottage, refusing to come in when Georgia called him.

'Whatever's the matter, Tru?' Georgia asked. Tru whined, running back and forth to the edge of the driveway. Following him, Georgia gasped at the sight of the large animal confronting her: a dog—no, it must be a lion—sat very still, looking at her with big brown eyes, while Tru ran circles around him.

'Is this your friend, Tru? Where did he come from?' Georgia carefully skirted the dog. He looked friendly enough, but his size was intimidating, and he had no collar or identification. As she was wondering what to do next, the local dog catcher drove up in a cloud of dust. The huge dog came to life, and he and Truman made a beeline into the house.

'Damn critter escaped this morning. Broke though the pound fence. Just took off. Must've known his days were numbered,' Jed, the dog catcher, said.

'What do you mean?' Georgia's eyes opened wide with anxiety.

'Well, he eats like a horse. Can't afford to keep him any longer,' Jed said. 'He was handed in when old Mr Grimshaw died last month. Had no place to go. No one wants a great big hulk, only the cute little fellas like your mista, lady.'

'You mean … you're gonna put him down?'

'Tomorrow's the day, ma'am.'

'I'll take him,' Georgia blurted. The words came out of her mouth before she could think about it.

'OK, ma'am, he's yours. But I warn you, he'll eat you outta house and home.'

Jed turned away, relieved to find the big lug a home. He wasn't an unkind man and didn't like putting an animal down, but the budget would only stretch so far and this one ate enough for four others.

'What's his name?' yelled Georgia after him.

'Scully. Good luck,' Jed replied.

Tru and Scully emerged cautiously as Jed drove off. Tru danced doughnuts around Scully, who looked at Georgia, and then came up to her and offered his right paw as if to say, 'Thanks.' She patted the big dog, a bit apprehensive about what she was going to do with him now that she had rescued him from death's jaws.

Feed him first, I guess.

She emptied a can of food into Tru's bowl. One gulp. It was gone.

Two cans … three cans … four cans … Finally, the Great Dane seemed satisfied—for now. 'Let's go for a walk, Tru. Bring your friend.'

Passing by the woodworks, she saw Gong Browne at the lathe. He often worked late, turning out his beautiful tables and chairs. He had more orders than he could keep up with. But he was always so sad, so lonely.

An idea struck Georgia.

'C'mon, you two, let's pay Gong a call.'

Entering the workroom, Tru rushed up to Gong, who was always happy to see him. As he leaned down to pet Tru, Scully came up behind him, startling the old carpenter.

'Where did you come from, big boy?' Gong exclaimed. Scully offered a paw silently, looking into his eyes. Gong's lower jaw trembled as he stared at the uplifted paw. The Great Dane waited patiently. Then Gong was on his knees hugging the dog.

Something happened. Man and dog seemed to find a common ground. For Scully, a new master, very much like the one he had lost; and for Gong, a friend to fill that lonely space in his heart.

Tru yapped his approval.

'He ran away from the pound,' Georgia explained. 'Scully was old Mr Grimshaw's dog. His fate was to be put down tomorrow, so I've taken him on. I guess it was a rather hasty decision and I'm not sure what to do with him now that I've rescued him.' Georgia frowned.

'Can't have that. He's still got plenty of life in him. He can stay in the barn,' Gong muttered gruffly.

Georgia looked back at them as she and Tru waved goodbye. Scully hadn't moved from under the bench at the old carpenter's feet. He'd found a home and a good master again.

It was the beginning of a warm and intimate friendship.

Together, Gong and Scully explored the community. They spent long hours walking through the forest and reflective moments on the banks of the stream, angling for tasty trout. They even started to attend Sunday services together, Gong sitting in a pew and Scully lying quietly at his feet.

Gong and Scully were inseparable over the next three years. Gong's loneliness faded, and he and Scully made many friends.

And Tru had found a friend—a big friend.

UNREST

The day dawned bright and sunny, the ideal day for a picnic or a day at the beach to celebrate Georgia's twenty-eighth birthday.

Georgia was awakened by Truman's cold wet nose nudging her, his big blue eyes fixed on her, begging her to wake up and play with him. She tossed her arm over to her husband's side of the bed to find it empty.

'Where is that man?' Georgia wondered with annoyance. Harry was a very early riser and usually up before 6 am, watering his beloved garden and talking to his roses. *He's probably out in the garden, as usual*, she thought.

'Go and play ball with your father, Tru,' Georgia, said, giving Tru a quick pat on the head. She rolled over, hoping to catch a few more minutes of shut-eye before leaving for work.

Married life had been happy, at first. She'd been busy, working hard to set up the beauty college. Her dedication had paid off and it was an outstanding success.

Students enjoyed a happy environment, and Georgia won the Business Woman of the Year Award this year, the college's third year in operation. She had matured and looked the embodiment of a successful career woman, elegant, slim, tall and impeccably groomed.

Harry was proud of his wife and always willing to help, from carting loads of towels to the laundromat to replacing light bulbs, fixing facial steamers and maintaining the large spa. He was hopelessly in love with his wife and his love knew no boundaries. Caring for her was his driving force, but he wondered sometimes whether it was a one-sided love.

Georgia seemed to have more affection for animals than humans, he thought—especially dogs. Yet there was something unawakened in his alluring wife, something she seemed to be endlessly searching for.

Georgia was bored.

Is this what life and marriage is all about? Where is all that fire and passion one reads about in romance novels? Harry is certainly stable, quiet and dependable, but romantic? No.

Her mind drifted back to Bombay … and Tics. What would it have been like to be married to him?

Truman's warm tongue licked a salty tear trickling down his mum's face and jolted her wide awake. Leaping out of bed, she looked at the clock, which showed 7 am.

'Oh my god, I'm gonna be late!' Tru looked at her reproachfully.

'Go find Dad, Tru. Remind him it's my birthday. I wonder if he even remembers.'

But the dog stayed faithfully at her bedside, settling down with a sigh. It didn't look as if there would be the ball game this morning that he was hanging out for.

Slipping on very high-heeled shoes—green designer stilettos—and swallowing down a glass of orange juice with a couple of vitamin tablets, Georgia gave the top of Tru's head a kiss. 'Promise to play ball this evening.'

Just as she grabbed her car keys off the kitchen counter, the back door slammed and Harry entered from the garden, wet and muddy.

Now running late for morning classes, Georgia was impatient and cross.

'Get those muddy boots off, Harry, and give Tru a bit of chicken for breakfast with some cheese on top.'

Harry nodded quietly and gave his wife a kiss on the cheek, but Georgia pulled away, slightly averting her face. She was annoyed and hurt that he didn't remember her birthday. If he did, surely he would wish her 'happy birthday', wouldn't he?

Irrationally, she lashed out. 'I'm late. Don't have time to take it easy like some people!'

Harry ignored his wife's outburst. It was no use wishing her a happy birthday given the mood she was in. Better save it for later, over a nice dinner and the present he had carefully chosen for her: an eternity ring set with blue sapphires to match the spaniel pendant, which she still always wore.

'Have a good day. How about a quiet dinner? I'll cook.'

'Your cooking—is that something to look forward to?' was her sarcastic reply. Blowing a kiss to Tru, Georgia dashed out the door.

Marking time at the traffic lights, Georgia drummed her fingers impatiently on the wheel. Just when she was in a hurry, they would take forever to change.

At last.

Accelerating hard, the heel of her right stiletto snapped off. Cursing, she stopped to pull off her outrageously expensive designer shoes and toss them into the back seat. Impatient drivers honked and hurled curses at her.

'Fuckin' hell, lady. What do you think this is? Fuckin' drivin' school? Get the hell outta here,' yelled a burly truck driver, coming up alongside and shaking his fist at her angrily.

Georgia raised her hand and gave him the finger, and then accelerated, burning rubber and narrowly missing a car.

A cop car.

Great. That was all she needed now.

Siren on, the cop signalled her to pull over.

'Lady, do you know you're ten miles per hour over the speed limit?'

'Shit! I'm late and my heel snapped.'

The tough old cop looked into the back seat of the car. 'Those killer heels will kill you one day. Licence, ma'am.'

He wrote a ticket and handed it to her through the car window.

She looked at it in amazement, exploding. 'One hundred dollars! Shit!'

'Move on, sweetheart, or I can keep adding—and I can only add in hundreds.'

'Thanks,' Georgia retorted angrily, but she didn't accelerate and spin off as she was tempted and risk any more trouble.

What a start to her birthday.

Parking her car, Georgia entered the front door of the college, brisk and authoritative—in stockinged feet, shoes in hand. She walked through racks of designer clothes, shoes and handbags, grabbing a pair of size 8 Jimmy Choo green stilettos on her way to her office.

Tossing her red shoes aside, she slipped on the new shoes almost without missing a beat in her stride.

Her staff greeted her as she walked by, but she simply nodded. They raised eyebrows, sensing she was not in a good mood today, and kept their distance.

Not Tanya, though.

Twenty-three-year-old Tanya, slightly autistic but wise beyond her years, had come to work at the college three years ago. She was the college housekeeper, gardener and keeper of the young students' hearts. Everyone loved her, though they couldn't always quite understand her. She had a rare way of expressing herself, which took some deciphering.

Tanya followed Georgia into her large office, a wide-open space of huge windows and streaming bright light, with an enormous black leather desk set at the end, near a bay window.

The distance from the entrance to the desk was intimidating, and her staff, when summoned, often felt they were 'walking the gangplank', not knowing what awaited them at the other end.

Georgia stood by the window, deep in thought. She touched her pendant, thinking back to that day when Harry bought her the necklace and her beloved dog, Truman.

It was the best birthday she'd ever had.

'Jor-gee.' Tanya's voice startled her, and she swung around. She had an affection for the youngest member of her staff. Tanya was worth her salt. No one wanted to employ her, the agency said, because of her 'fault'. It seemed both dogs and humans with 'faults' came close to perfect in Georgia's book.

'What is it, Tanya?' Georgia smiled for the first time that day.

'Well, I just wanted to show you my ring. Lang and me are engaged to live together now,' Tanya bubbled, flashing her hand with a modest but exquisite antique sapphire and diamond ring set in yellow gold.

'Oh, I see,' Georgia replied cautiously. 'You mean you're getting married? It's a gorgeous ring, Tanya!'

'He'll have to ask me about that. He's only asked me to get engaged, and I said I'm not having no babies as yet either.'

'No, of course not,' Georgia replied seriously.

'And this is for you.' Tanya laid a small box wrapped with red ribbon on Georgia's desk. 'Happy day of your birth.'

Suddenly Tanya, looking out of the window, gasped and, before Georgia could thank her, she exclaimed, 'I must go and water the garden before the rain catches up. The thunder clouds are coming.' And off she dashed, leaving Georgia amused, but feeling much better. Tanya could always make people feel good, with her effusiveness, vibrant energy and quirky expressions of love.

Someone remembered her Day of Birth.

She looked at the little box, so carefully wrapped in yellow tissue paper saved from presents gone before, and the red ribbon, slightly worn—so full of love. A white lace handkerchief embroidered with a black-and-white, blue-eyed cocker spaniel in the corner, hand sewn and beautiful, lay in the box. Tears welled up in Georgia's eyes as she gazed at those sad blue eyes.

The handkerchief came to good use.

'Good morning, Georgia.' Lauren placed a cup of tea on her desk.

'Thanks.' Georgia smiled. She had regained her composure and the brisk business woman turned towards her secretary, ready for the day.

'On the agenda today, your appointment to orientate Michelle Stamford, the new make-up artistry teacher, is at 1 pm, Jenny and Toni have called in sick and the new make-up products haven't arrived.'

'What! Sick? They'd better be dying! Too much of last night's one-night stands, I bet,' Georgia interrupted.

'And you're teaching the structure of the skin in morning class,' Lauren calmly continued.

Students filled the classroom, many chattering as only young girls can.

'Good morning, ladies, and Henry,' Georgia greeted her new fledglings.

Henry had taken a seat next to Eileen and looked quite at home with all the females.

'Good morning, Georgia,' was the unanimous chorus, as chairs scraped and skirts rustled. They all looked immaculate and very ladylike in their grey skirts and pink blouses, embroidered with the college logo. Black ballet pumps and stockings completed the uniform. Georgia had modified the uniform for Henry, and he looked sharp in a pink shirt, grey trousers and black shoes.

Georgia commenced writing on the whiteboard.

'Today, we're going to learn the structure of the skin and the ageing process.'

It was a busy day training the students in skin care, dress sense and make-up. In facial class, students lay on couches prepared for facial treatments as others worked on them. Georgia demonstrated different facial massage techniques.

Next it was fashion class. Each of the students had changed from their uniform to a favourite outfit they'd brought from home, and Georgia critiqued them. They were often mismatched or unflattering, and Georgia offered solutions to better co-ordinate the outfits.

One eighteen-year-old, wearing a dull-green skirt and patterned blouse, was shown how a jacket—Georgia grabbed a lovely, khaki classic blazer and helped the student into it—could complete an outfit.

Make-up class was the last class of the day, and Georgia hoped the new teacher would be good. It would help reduce Georgia's practical teaching workload and free her up to work on other aspects of the business, which was growing rapidly.

As usual, the younger girls plastered on heavy make-up, looking garish and crude. Georgia painstakingly demonstrated a light make-up for day wear.

It was 1:15 pm, and students tidied up and prepared to leave, while Tanya buzzed around like a mother hen, supervising the clean-up. The younger girls hated cleaning up, like most young girls, but nothing escaped Tanya's eagle eye and they wouldn't be allowed to leave till their workstations were shipshape.

As Tanya started folding towels and wiping down a couch, she snapped, 'C'mon then, ladies, or I'll be mad as a cut snake!'

Everyone sprang into action and soon the job was complete.

Georgia was tired. She was seriously considering taking an early mark and shelving the paperwork for the day, when Lauren popped her head around the door.

'Michelle Stamford is here.'

Damn. She had forgotten her. 'Come in, Michelle.'

Michelle entered hesitantly and said, 'Good afternoon, Mrs Haines.'

'Call me Georgia. Sit down. You have an impressive résumé: Paris, New York, Japanese Shisedo make-up. Michelle, your initiation class is tomorrow. I want you to teach the students basic make-up, a non-formal face: matte foundation under a slight brush of bronze powder, a light dab of liquid or cream blush, some very sexy dark-lined eyes and a high-gloss lip colour—comprehend?'

'No problem.'

'You'll be on trial for one week; non-performance will get you a walking ticket.'

'You'll be pleased with my work, Georgia. Thank you for giving me the chance,' Michelle replied, undaunted.

Georgia looked at her quizzically over her large Dior spectacles.

Georgia decided to leave early, taking advantage of the half day, along with her students. It was her birthday, after all.

Changing her stilettos for walking shoes and her Gucci suit for jeans and a jacket, Georgia decided to take a drive down to the coast. Harry would be at the office all day, and she could do with a breath of fresh sea air and some time to herself to clear her head.

DEVIL IN DISGUISE

The winding road down to Bateman's Bay was a pleasant drive, with not much traffic on the road in the middle of the afternoon on a weekday. She slipped an Elvis album into the player and sang along to 'Devil in Disguise':

You look like an angel,
Walk like an angel,
Talk like an angel,
But I got wise,
You're the devil in disguise.

Georgia wondered if she was a devil in disguise—something was missing.

Was there more to life than this? She had a flourishing business, a husband that loved her ... Why wasn't she satisfied? Where did true happiness lie? On this, her twenty-eighth birthday, she felt alone and lost. She craved more excitement.

Harry was so predictable. It would just be another boring evening, anyway, with Harry cooking a meal. He hadn't even remembered her birthday—not even a phone call. She forgot, of course, that she had instructed him never to call her during lectures, unless it was a matter of life and death.

The late afternoon sun was pleasant, but there was a chill in the air. Georgia wrapped the red wool scarf closer around her neck. As she approached, she noticed Lang, Tanya's boyfriend, and his border-collie Labrador-cross, Nugget, riding the waves. Lang was a nice boy, studying to be a doctor. Nugget was a star attraction, and they were out together most days, to the delight of an ever-growing and appreciative new audience of locals and visitors.

Lang and his dog surfing together was an eye-catching act. They seemed to anticipate one another's moves, neither getting wet as they caught and rode the waves at will, each time calmly exiting in unbroken water to paddle the hundred metres back to await their next big ride.

On the way out, Nugget stood tall, almost hanging-ten on the nose of the board, providing balance for Lang's paddling. Then, once they were on the wave, Nugget slipped back half a metre to squat in a unique and anything but your normal backside-on-the-ground doggie pose, as if to provide the best possible balance for the thrilling wave-riding journey.

The big board glided along the wave, rising gently to the crest, and then zipped down the face before exiting closer to the beach. Its riders turned around and did it all again.

Inexplicably, Nugget suddenly decided to ride backwards for a few strokes, looking back at his master as if to say, 'Was that all right?' So, on the next ride, Lang, using doggie psychology, returned the compliment by turning his back on Nugget to ride the wave backwards.

It was all part of the extraordinary synergy between the two. For those watching from surfboards nearby or on the shore, it was a fascinating free-of-charge exhibition of tandem, stand-up paddle-boarding and super-dog performance … a real tail-wagger.

Georgia strolled along the beach, barefoot, her toes curling in the sand. She wondered what the real meaning of life was. One of her students, Mariah, who was a psychic and very spiritual, kept talking about this 'inner peace' one could reach, which was all-fulfilling. How did one get there? Did one have to meditate on a mountaintop?

Mother Meg seemed to have it, but she didn't achieve it that way. 'Just be yourself; don't try to be what you're not,' Mother Meg said.

All her life she had tried to be what her parents expected of her, tried awfully hard to please them. Wasn't that what one was supposed to do?

Oh, damn, think I'll go for a swim, Georgia thought. *The water is always warmer than the air.*

Stripping down to her bathers under her jeans and jacket, Georgia ventured into the waves. After the first gasp, as the cold water hit her, she felt invigorated and started a steady breaststroke out towards the sea. Flipping over on her back to float for a while, she noticed old Gong and Scully on the beach. The great big hound was splashing just offshore, almost making waves as big as the surf as he ploughed through the water after an elusive ball bobbing on the waves.

Turning over, Georgia felt exhilarated and, deciding to swim out further, picked up a steady over-arm stroke. She used to enter all the swimming competitions at school and won a few medals. The afternoon sun was setting, low beyond the horizon, as she swam out to sea, and she was totally oblivious to the fact that she had passed the safe area between the flags.

The water felt balmy now, like a soothing cocoon around her. The sun sparkled on the water like a million leadlight crystals bursting out with light.

On and on, right arm over left, strong leg muscles performing precision scissor strokes, her lithe body propelled itself through the water effortlessly.

Then … Wham! … She felt a huge pull and got caught in the rip that appeared out of nowhere.

Don't panic, tread water, swim parallel to shore and call for help, the voice of her swimming coach rang around in her head.

'Help, over here,' she called, waving her arms wildly. The sea was silent, Georgia was getting tired. Everything started turning dark, and her legs and arms felt like jelly. She felt the panic rising and tried desperately to swim parallel to the shore, but she was still in a strong current and exhaustion threatened to overcome her.

Suddenly, a huge animal lifted her from under the waves.

Oh, my god, a shark, flashed through her mind, as her arms automatically grabbed the body of the creature. Fur? A shark didn't have fur … Must be the Loch Ness sea monster. She hung on for dear life as she was torpedoed through the water and deposited unceremoniously on the sand, gasping and sputtering. A cold wet nose nudged her, and a loud bark greeted her.

Scully … The Great Dane had saved her life.

The nurse handed her a steaming cup of tea. Taking it gratefully, she looked at old Gong's worried face at her bedside.

'Thought we'd lost you there, young lass,' he muttered gruffly.

'I'm all right.' Georgia rested a kind hand on the old man's arm. 'Thanks to that big lug of a mutt.'

'Called Harry, I did. He'll be down soon.'

He'll be cross, Georgia thought; swimming out to sea past the flag lines … I'll have to face the music.

Harry rushed in just then, worry written all over his face. Gong silently left the room, leaving the young couple alone.

Without a word, Harry wrapped his arms around his wife and held her close. She was safe and sound—that was all that mattered.

The next morning, as Harry and Georgia drove up the pathway to Carpenter's Cottage, Truman raced out of the doggie flap like a bullet. Mum was home. All was right in his world. Burnt out embers of a log fire, a candle on the dining table set for two, and a card and tiny gift-wrapped box on Georgia's plate, next to a wilting red rose, said it all.

A birthday remembered.

'I'll make us some breakfast, while you have a hot shower and get into bed, *buddhi*,' Harry called out, heading for the kitchen.

He hadn't called her that old pet name for a long time. It was one of the endearing terms they had for each other, *buddhi* and *buddha*—old girl and old boy—from their Indian heritage.

LOVE HAS NO LABELS

As the year progressed, Georgia watched her charges become more proficient at their treatments and hone their skills. It was her passion to train good therapists and see them well employed in the beauty industry or setting up their own salons. She would continue mentoring them in the initial years of business and take great pride in her new graduates and their successes. A support group for past graduates was formed by the student body and met every second Tuesday of the month to discuss new innovations in the industry, brainstorm ideas and share challenges and solutions.

Henry fitted in well with everyone, and they loved him like a big brother. Everyone wanted to partner with him when it came time for practical work. They said he had the gentlest hands and his facial treatments were the best. He certainly was very attentive in class and followed instructions to the letter, often offering his opinion or doing something in a new and innovative way. Everyone formed their little friendships during the year, and Henry and Eileen seemed to have formed a bond of sorts. He was very protective of her.

One afternoon, a rough-looking tattooed guy with shoulder-length hair was waiting at the front door of the college as Eileen emerged after class.

'C'mon, baby, you're late. Been waiting twenty minutes,' he said, grabbing her arm roughly. Eileen flinched and drew away.

'This guy botherin' you, Eileen?' Henry asked as he loomed over the tattooed bloke. Henry was three inches over six feet tall, and of no puny build—enough to scare the daylights out of anyone who didn't know the gentle giant.

'It's all right, Henry.' Eileen smiled weakly up at him. 'Let's go, Jake.'

'Who's the big oaf? Another of your tricks?' Jake sneered.

Eileen had confided in Lauren that she was a 'gentleman's companion', she said, to put it nicely. The work paid good money and she was able to keep her kids in school and cared for very well. She would give it up when she qualified and could work as a beauty therapist. Eileen had begged Lauren not to disclose her secret to the other students. She had been scared to say what her profession was in case she was judged and refused entry to the college.

As the year flew by and everyone slowly became professionally skilled, Georgia and the other girls could see that Henry worshipped the ground Eileen walked on. Georgia often saw them down the beach with Eileen's four kids: twin seven-year-old boys, Jack and Andrew; a ten-year-old girl, Jamie; and twelve-year-old, Kevin.

Tanya and Lang, and their dog, Nugget, had struck up a friendship with them, and Lang often allowed Kevin to surf on his board with him, patiently waiting when Kevin fell off over and over again as he learned to balance on the board.

'They'd make a hooley dooley pair,' Tanya, a born matchmaker said, shaking her head wisely. 'Eileen needs someone to look after her real proper.'

Henry would certainly have agreed and stepped into the role quite readily, but did Eileen like him? Georgia couldn't get too involved in the personal lives of her students. She had to concentrate on training them to the highest level, to launch them on their career. But there were always certain students that found a place into her heart, and Eileen and Henry were certainly two of them.

Then there was young Trudy. She walked with a limp, having suffered from polio, which left her right leg shorter than the other and emaciated. On excursions, she found it hard to keep up with the others, and big-hearted Henry always lagged behind to keep her company. When it came time to learn the faradic muscle exercising machine for stomach tightening, butt lifting and thigh firming, Henry strapped the machine onto Trudy's legs and faithfully treated and massaged her wasted limb each day. By the end of the year, Trudy's right leg had strengthened and filled out. Despite its shortness, she was walking with a spring in her step.

Henry was Trudy's idol—she followed him around everywhere. He didn't seem to mind. All the clients in the student salon asked Henry for facial treatments.

'That male therapist has the gentlest and most skilled hands,' they said.

It was autumn again, and Eileen and Henry walked hand in hand through the thick carpets of leaves on the ground. Truman, who also thought the world of Henry, was often at their side, prancing and rolling around in the dry leaves, with the twins following on their bikes. They were falling deeply in love, but Eileen hadn't told him about her secret life.

Till one day it all came to a head: the police came to the college asking for Eileen. 'We need Eileen to come down to the police station,' Constable McCarthy said.

Lauren called Eileen out of class, and Henry, very worried, followed them to the office.

'Do you have someone to accompany you to the police station, ma'am?' the young copper asked.

'Yes—me,' Henry answered firmly, despite Eileen's protests. 'Let's go.'

At the precinct, Eileen was needed to identify the 'client' that had physically abused her the night before. The owner of the parlour had reported it when Eileen came out, bruised and hysterical, from her room.

She had covered the bruises on her arms with long sleeves, and the large bruise on her cheek with heavy make-up, saying she had tripped and hit her face on the floor. Nervously scanning the eight faces in the line-up behind the one-way glass, Eileen confidently pointed to the man at the end of the line.

'Yes, that's him.' Eileen identified the guy with the tattooed arms.

As Jake was escorted out, handcuffed, he sneered at Eileen and Henry. 'You can have her, mister, for what she's worth.'

Henry jumped at Jake angrily, swinging a punch at him, but was quickly restrained by two policemen.

'OK, ma'am, you may go,' Constable McCarthy said. 'Just sign the ID papers on the way out.'

Henry took Eileen to the 'Ladies A-Waiting' parlour to collect her things, telling her firmly she was not going back. It was only a couple of months to graduation, and he was already setting up his practice. He wanted her to work with him and move to Sydney. It would be good for her to get away from Canberra and the regrettable memories it held.

The boys could go to Sydney Grammar, his Alma Mater, he said.

Eileen wanted the brothel to be nothing more than a faded memory. Its empty walls and dark interior made the company there seem even more sinister. The women were nothing but goods and chattels. They could be pushed around as long as the clients kept coming back. Henry was shaking as they stepped through the front door.

They walked through the house, which contained differently themed rooms, including a 'torture chamber' complete with whips, handcuffs, and ropes, a 'dress-up party room' and the 'little boys' room. The doors had no knobs. The sounds Henry heard through the walls made him blush and begin to sweat. Eileen eyed him carefully, trying to see what he was thinking.

They walked upstairs to a dorm. Small suitcases were strewn across the floor. Dressers exploded with clothes. It seemed some had been there for days, others for years. The class of the women surprised Henry. He did not expect to see young and innocent-looking beautiful faces. Girls were whispering in the hallway. They smiled at first when they saw Eileen and then stared wide-eyed at Henry. Henry felt sick to the stomach thinking of Eileen working there. There was nothing for her there. Young girls eyed him curiously; he didn't seem to fit the bill of a client. They gathered he was a friend of Eileen's.

'Where ya goin', Eileen?' Jess asked, seeing Eileen pack her suitcase.

'Outta here, just outta here,' Henry replied.

Late that evening, after the kids had gone to bed, Henry and Eileen sat before an open fire, Nugget at their feet. Tanya and Lang were away for the weekend and they were dog-sitting.

'Why didn't you tell me, Eileen?' Henry asked gently.

'I was so ashamed,' she answered. 'I didn't know what to do when Jack died. He was a good father and husband. It was all so sudden. His heart just stopped. They didn't know why. Jack was always healthy and active, till one day he sat in this chair and never got up.'

The dam of tears waiting to be released broke, and Eileen burst into tears, crying her heart out. Henry held her, rocking her gently.

'Shush,' he said softly. 'I'm going to take care of you now.'

'No man would want a ready-made family of four kids and a tarnished woman.' Eileen sobbed with a big hiccup.

Offering her a large white handkerchief, Henry held her close.

'This man wants you and your four kids—that is, if you want him. I love you, Eileen.'

'I love you too, Henry,' she murmured, looking up at him with so much love in her eyes his heart skipped a beat.

As he enfolded her in his arms, the autumn leaves fell and the gusts of wind blew them against the window pane—red, yellow, orange and green.

Nugget snored and rolled over, four legs in the air, toasted and warm.

Eileen had found her haven and Henry his 'pretty woman', to take care of for the rest of their lives.

Tyler and Bert were a couple. They loved to come and chat to the students at the salon, while they had their nails manicured, feet scrubbed and faces masqued. Girl talk was the highlight of their day.

Tanya loved them, and they her. Often they could be seen out in the garden, in their white, terrycloth bathrobes, on their 'spa day', sipping green tea and partaking of an egg Caesar salad for lunch.

'Bert refuses to give me an extra fifty dollars housekeeping money,' Tyler said crossly. 'We never have prawns for entrée, which I luuuve!'

'You're a silly prawn yourself,' Bert chided good naturedly. 'All right, if you must have it—but you'll have to cut your spa day.'

'Never!' Tyler gasped. He loved coming to the salon. It made his day. 'My skin will go all wrinkly, like a prawn.'

'Prawns or wrinkles; your choice!'

Before the argument got out of hand, Tanya piped up. 'Laugh a lot, and when you're older, all your wrinkles will be in the right places.'

God love her, she always knew the right thing to say—in Tanya style.

One day, Tanya came to Georgia's office, her face mirroring her deep anguish.

'Tyler has been diagnosed with cancer. Bert says he only has four months to live … and he can have prawns every day.' Tanya sobbed.

Georgia hugged her young staff member. Tanya was the most loving, compassionate soul in the world. Lang was a lucky man, and Georgia hoped he realised it and proposed soon.

Some days Tyler just came to lie in the spa after his chemotherapy and sip green tea. Bert never left his side.

There wasn't a more loving couple … and Tanya watched over them like a mother hen.

TANYA GETS MARRIED

'Hi, Jor-gee.' Tanya poked her head around Georgia's office door one morning.

'Good morning, Tanya. How's that young man of yours?'

'Lang, well he wants to get married soon. I said yes, cuz then I'll have someone to fall asleep with.'

'When?'

'Next week. We want Tyler and Bert to be able to come.'

Georgia did a double take. 'What! Have you organised outfits, bridesmaids, best man, your dress …' Georgia's voice trailed off.

'I was wonderin' if you could help with all that, you knowing about the high and low fashion and stuff,' Tanya replied nonchalantly.

'Get them all here this afternoon, pronto, Tanya,' Georgia exclaimed. 'We'd better get on to it; there's no time to waste.'

In a flurry of excitement, Lauren and Georgia rushed downtown and returned with an assortment of outfits suitable for bridesmaids, suits for the best man and some stunning wedding dresses for Tanya to choose from. The boutiques were ready to help when Georgia explained the situation. Everyone in the township loved Tanya.

'Look!' Lauren exclaimed, pointing out the bay window.

Arriving in Lang's truck were the best man and bridesmaids.

'Tyler and Bert, my best friends, are my bridesmaids,' Tanya said, and turned to introduce the third member of the party.

'Kelly is Lang's sister. She's the best man. Real butch she is, too.'

'How exciting! I love a dress up, don't you?' Tyler said with a smile.

'More suits, Lauren. There's a change of plans.' Georgia raised her eyebrows in amusement. 'And those frilled blouses, the lavender ones. Also, the pin-striped with the lavender shirt and grey silk tie.'

The afternoon was a whirl of trying on outfits, facials, and manicures. Tanya looked exquisite in a soft, romantic A-line gown with asymmetrical ruching. It was elegant and flowy, with white roses sewn on the skirt.

'Lang will think I look like a wedding cake and might want to eat me,' she said innocently, to roars of laughter.

'Cake!' Georgia was aghast. 'Have we ordered a cake?'

'I'll take care of everything,' Lauren assured her.

The day of the wedding dawned bright and clear. The bridesmaids, in their steel-grey suits and ruffled lavender blouses, with sprigs of lavender in their lapels, looked a picture. Kelly, in her pin-striped, light-grey suit, purple shirt and silver tie, was a dapper best man.

And Tanya … Well, Tanya was an absolute vision in tiers of lace and satin, carrying a bouquet of white roses, calla lily and lavender with baby's breath. Her veil covered a sweet face that radiated kindness and love for the man she was about to give her life to.

Scully and Nugget, in lavender waistcoats, lay side by side under Gong's pew, wondering what all the fuss was about. *If a dog wants a mate, that's it; he finds one,* they seemed to be saying. *But humans have to have all the fanfare. Oh well, that's their way. Let's have a snooze. Might be some good tucker later.*

The minister commenced the ceremony. 'Be who God meant you to be and you will set the world on fire. Marriage is intended to be a way in which man and woman help each other to become what God intended, their deepest and truest selves. Marriage should transform, as husband and wife make one another their work of art. Each must give the other space and freedom.

'Lang, you may now say your wedding vows.'

Lang blushed a bright red and looked at Tanya with the eyes of a man smitten for life.

'From this moment, I, Lang, take you, Tanya, as my best friend for life. I pledge to honour, encourage, and support you through our walk together. When our way becomes difficult, I promise to stand by you and uplift you, so that through our union we can accomplish more than we could do alone. I promise to work at our love and always make you a priority in my life. With every beat of my heart, I will love you. This is my solemn vow.'

Georgia, standing next to Harry, accepted his hand in hers as tears welled in her eyes.

'You may say your vows now, Tanya.' The minister smiled at her.

'I, Tanya, take you, Lang, as the love of my life. I vow to be patient with you and the circumstances in our lives. I vow to be kind to all people we come across. I promise not to be quick to anger, but to think before I speak and act. I vow not to keep a record of wrongs, but to always keep the happy memories alive. Through God, our love will never fail …

and I will wash your socks and make your favourite shepherd's pie.'

The grounds of Carpenter's Cottage had never looked more charming than this evening. As the fairy lights amongst the trees twinkled and the haunting strains of Beethoven's 'Moonlight Sonata' fill the air, Gong Browne remembered the day he married his young bride. Martha was the most angelic bride in the world. Their love had lasted a lifetime. She was gone now, but the memories they had made together would always be in his heart. His hand moved down to pat Scully's head. The Great Dane looked up at him with eyes that said, *I know; I'm here for you. I love you with all my doggy heart.*

Tyler and Bert had their arms around each other's shoulders, their heads leaning together. Whatever the future might bring, they were together, for now and till death did they part.

Tanya and Lang were married.

Georgia, watching the happy young couple, wondered why she had been feeling so dissatisfied lately, while Harry simply worried about keeping the woman he adored.

Scully and Nugget got a sausage each and were off by the stream to chase a rabbit or maybe catch a trout or two.

TRUMAN

Four years later ...

After Georgia left to lecture a business class, Harry and Truman progressed with their day.

Harry made a cup of tea and toast, buttered with Vegemite and topped with cheese, as Truman watched expectantly, drooling.

'Don't tell your mum what you had for breakfast. You'll get me in trouble.' Harry grinned as he gave him a slice of toast with some topping. Tru scoffed the toast, wagging his tail happily.

'Well, what should we have for dinner? My culinary expertise is limited. Any suggestions?' He talked to the dog as he looked in the freezer. Tru cocked his head as if thinking.

'Hmm ... we'll see. Let's go and prune the roses.'

Tru loved gardening with his dad. He dropped his ball at his feet in anticipation, waiting for Harry to hit it so they could play a game of hide and seek. Harry, digging a hole to plant a new rosebush, resurrected an old bone. Tru grabbed his treasure and rushed off to bury it elsewhere, looking furtively to see if his father was watching.

'We'd better get going, Tru,' Harry said, looking at his watch. It was nearly 11:00 am. Tru's work was to visit a local assisted-living centre with memory-impaired residents. The dear old folks took him for walks around their outdoor courtyard and played fetch with him on their grassy knoll.

Tru visited the elderly bed-ridden residents in their rooms and waited for his blanket to be laid on their bed, so he could jump up and cuddle them. These people had difficulty remembering family, but they always instantly recognised Truman and welcomed him with open arms and kisses.

'What a beautiful dress you wear,' exclaimed Mrs Stephanopoulos, an eighty-year-old Greek lady, looking at Truman's distinct markings.

Arriving home, Harry looked at the time.

'Just time to shower and change for my 3:30 pm meeting, Tru. You can have a nice chicken wing and a snooze till Mum gets home. Think that's a good idea?'

Tru wagged in assent. He loved his visits to the elderly citizens with his dad, but home and sustenance after his tiring morning sounded good.

Harry found a chicken wing for Tru, who polished it off in a flash and headed for his basket, scrunching in comfortably.

'Well, better get my skates on,' Harry said. 'It's nearly three o'clock.' Tru raised an eyebrow, already half in the land of nod.

Wonderful ability dogs have of switching off instantly and relaxing, Harry thought. *Wish humans could do just that. The world would be a less stressful place.*

As the razor stroked streams of lather in precise lines down his strong dark skin, Harry's mind flashed back to the day he first met Georgia at his best friend Darryl's birthday party.

Life together for the first five years was deliriously happy. Tru grew into a handsome dog and Georgia showed him at the local championships. The dog that breeders rejected as a show dog won first prize in his category. Harry and Georgia proudly brought Truman's trophy and ribbon home, placing it in pride of place on the mantelpiece.

Harry remembered their beautiful life of togetherness, the long walks they took in the park, hand in hand, sitting down to a picnic basket in the grass. In love, and carefree.

Truman took advantage and, while they were engrossed in a deep kiss, sneaked a ham sandwich from the hamper.

The holidays by the seaside, snorkelling in the ocean, with Truman chasing that elusive bobbing ball on the waves. Lang, Tanya and Nugget often joined them, and they all spent many a lazy afternoon watching Lang and Nugget show off their prowess on a surfboard.

Gong and Scully also walked the beach, and when all three dog friends met, they carried on like all their Christmases had come at once, chasing balls and digging in the sand, to be taken home a soggy, sandy mess, but ecstatic.

It was a dog's life and Harry's living dream.

Then things started to change.

Georgia seemed to grow restless. She had a passion for life, and everything she did was wholehearted and time consuming. She loved her business, which she had constructed from scratch, nurturing it from a baby into an award-winning college. The college had a waiting list, with women from the age of sixteen to forty knocking down the doors to get in, and the beauty salon attached to the college was the most popular in the city. It was always booked out. The salon gave the students a good grounding experience and launch pad for their future beauty careers, and the clients received advantageous treatment at a reasonable price. It was a win-win situation for all.

Georgia put her life and soul into the college, and was away more and more, at seminars interstate and overseas— New York, Paris and Milan—learning new arts of beauty and implementing them at her college. She had a driving force to achieve.

Georgia's parents constantly travelled, and when they were in town, the attempts she made to visit them usually ended in frustration and more withdrawal.

Harry kept the home fires burning and spent many lonely evenings with Tru at his feet by the fireside. Two pairs of eyes would light up as they heard Georgia's key turn in the lock. She was usually tired at the end of a busy day and, with a kiss on the top of two heads, tumbled into bed.

Harry felt lonely and isolated as the years passed. He thought about the promotion. The promotion he had turned down several years ago. If he had accepted, would she have come with him? The United States was a whole new kettle of fish. Georgia would feel as if he had forced her to abandon her life. Yet maybe she would not be as distant. Her life would be less busy, and maybe she would realise how lonely he felt. But her life was how she wanted it, and he was proud of her drive and passion. Harry swallowed hard at the thought of what they used to be like. Georgia's passion for the college was the passion she used to share with him. He missed it. The way she would wake him up by kissing his neck or wrapping her arms around him. When they cooked and danced together in the kitchen while Elvis played in the background, or when they travelled on the road together and talked about life and love. There was no time for that now, but Harry could not give up hope that it would return someday.

For now, he only hoped.

Tru's loud barking jolted him out of his reverie. The dog had spotted the neighbour's cat on his backyard fence. Jumping up, front paws scratching the fence, Tru was clearly saying, 'Out of here! This is my territory!'

Totally unafraid and nonchalant, the cat jumped down, almost landing on Tru's back. With a yelp, he turned and ran helter-skelter through his doggie flap into the kitchen, scattering his water bowl with a huge splash. What a hero!

Typical male when confronted by an alluring foxy feline, Harry thought wryly.

'Tru, you're a character! I'm off. See you this evening,' Harry said, patting him. 'Go back to sleep.'

Turning to grab the car keys and dash out the garage, he remembered the sandwiches Georgia had made him the night before for lunch. He'd better get them from the fridge, or she'd be cross.

Running late now, he opened the garage door and waved to Roy, his neighbour, a paramedic, trimming his front hedge. Tru had followed him out, panting for breath.

'Tru, you silly sausage. Teach you to try to get the better of a woman,' Harry said. 'No more feline chasing for the rest of the day. You can't win, you know.'

Truman collapsed.

Alarm washed over Harry's face. Feeling Tru's pulse, he found it low. The dog was failing.

'Heart attack?' He didn't realise he had spoken out loud and was startled by Roy's voice.

'Dogs don't have heart attacks. It could be a stroke or epileptic fit,' Roy said. 'Get him to the vet.'

Picking up Tru, Harry and Roy laid him carefully on the back seat of the car. 'Thanks, man. I'll dash him to Dr Payton.'

Harry burst in the front door of All Creatures Great and Small Veterinary Practice carrying a limp Tru.

'Good morning, Mr Haines,' the startled young receptionist, Jenny, greeted him.

'Tru's collapsed. He's dying, quick … Oh, please!'

'Calm down, Mr Haines. We'll attend to him immediately,' Jenny assured him, calling emergency on the intercom. A nurse and young doctor appeared and took Truman away.

Harry sat nervously drumming fingers in the waiting room. It had only been twenty minutes, but it seemed like hours. It was a busy day at the animal surgery, and a constant stream of animal lovers arrived with their dogs and cats for consultations.

A lady sat next to Harry with her pet python in a glass case. 'Slip has something stuck in his stomach,' she informed Harry.

After what seemed an eternity, Dr Payton—the senior vet, who owned the practice and knew Tru well—emerged.

'You'll need to leave him with us for a while. He's on a drip. A few moments later and the dog might not have lived.'

'What happened? Truman was fine chasing a cat …'

Dr Payton rested a kindly hand on his shoulder. 'I need to run some tests. Call me in about an hour.'

'I'd like to wait, Dr Payton. And I must inform my wife. May I use your phone?'

'As you wish,' the kindly doctor replied and showed Harry into his office.

Harry dialled Georgia's college.

'I must speak to my wife! It's urgent,' he informed Lauren, who answered the phone.

'She's in the midst of a lecture. Can I give her a message?'

'Interrupt.'

Georgia's voice was cross over the telephone.

'It'd better be a matter of life and death. Didn't I tell you not to disturb me during lectures? Don't you ever listen?'

'Something terrible happened. It's Tru—'

'Oh, my god, my baby son—' Georgia's voice broke as she struggled to speak.

'Tru collapsed. I'm at Dr Payton's.'

'What … What did you do? Can't you do anything right? I'll be there in ten minutes.' The phone slammed down in his ear.

Harry couldn't stand his wife being upset. Truman was her life. She lived for her dog. 'I love that dog more than anyone in the world,' she often said.

That included him as well, he surmised.

Harry stepped out into the courtyard. In the afternoon sunshine, it was exercise time for the dogs in boarding, who were running around chasing balls and jumping through hoops. Truman was doing just that a short time ago, chasing a cat. Georgia would be beside herself. He'd better prepare for what was to come.

'Where's my son? Where's Tru? I want to see him now.' Georgia burst into the veterinary practice and rushed up to the reception desk, ignoring other waiting customers.

'The vet will be with you shortly,' replied the young receptionist efficiently. 'Please have a seat, Mrs Haines.'

Harry whispered to Georgia, telling her of the events leading up to Tru's collapse. She was too upset and beyond speech at this stage even to reprimand her husband any further. He attempted to put an arm around her in comfort, but she shrugged it off impatiently.

Just then Dr Payton strode briskly into the room. 'Come with me.'

Tru was in the surgery, a forlorn little figure with a drip in his right leg. He looked lifeless. Georgia was beside herself.

'Tru, my baby, my son,' she murmured as she showered little kisses all over his face and stroked his velvet ears.

'He's extremely sick indeed, Mrs Haines. If your husband hadn't got him here in time, he might not have lived,' Dr Payton said seriously.

'What's the matter with my boy, Dr Payton?' she asked.

'I need to run some more tests and an ultrasound. His calcium levels are high. Worst case scenario: cancer. I'm sorry.'

'But he was chasing a cat this morning,' Harry exclaimed.

'These things come on without any warning in dogs. They're such happy, loving beings and never complain. Look at him now, not a whimper, though he's in a great deal of pain.'

Georgia was in a state of shock, silent tears rolling down her face.

'My baby, I love you, please don't die,' she whispered, kneeling down to Tru.

Dr Payton gently lifted her up. 'You must go home now. He's in good care. I'll call you in the morning.'

'Can't I take him home and bring him back tomorrow?' she begged.

'You can do as you please. He's your dog, but I wouldn't advise it.'

'We'll leave him in your good hands, Dr Payton.' Harry shook the vet's hand.

Georgia turned back and kissed Tru once more, before she reluctantly allowed Harry to guide her firmly out of the surgery.

At 9:00 am the next day, Harry brought his wife a breakfast tray and opened the window blinds, letting in the morning sunshine. She'd had a restless night, only falling into a deep sleep at around 3:00 am, probably from sheer exhaustion.

He'd let her sleep in. There was no Tru this morning, with his wet cold nose to nudge her awake, and their appointment with the vet was not until 11:30 am. She'd have ample time to shower and change after breakfast, before going down to the surgery.

Lauren was coping with the students and Michelle, the new teacher, was doing well at her new teaching post, so there was no need for Georgia to go into the college today. He was not sure she could anyway. As resilient as she was, Truman's illness had devastated her.

'Thank you,' Georgia said simply, picking at her toast. The tea would warm her up and she seemed to be grateful as she cupped her hands around the mug and sipped slowly. This all seemed so surreal. Tru was bouncing around full of life, tail wagging and long silky ears flying, only yesterday, and today he was lying at death's door.

Life changes in an instant.

Meeting with the radiologist, Dr Nanette, a brusque woman in her mid-sixties, Harry and Georgia sat on the edge of their seats, awaiting the verdict.

'Dr Payton asked me to do an ultrasound on your dog. I'm afraid the news isn't good. Your dog, Truman, has cancer of the liver. One large tumour, and the whole liver is shot to pieces. Bluntly, he has a matter of weeks to live, maybe a month,' Dr Nanette said, frankly. She loved animals and hated passing on bad news to her patients, but she didn't beat around the bush and always gave it to them straight, without raising false hopes. She had seen many cases of this type of cancer in cocker spaniels and it was terminal.

'No, no, it can't be!' Georgia cried.

Harry put an arm around his wife as Dr Nanette continued, 'I'll give you some medication, pain-killers, to ease the pain and you can take him home. There's nothing more we can do for the dog here. You'll need to make the decision to give him his final injection soon, which I recommend, as the pain starts causing too much suffering in the animal. The psyche also gets unstable and unpredictable.'

'Absolutely not!' Georgia was distraught.

'Thank you for being so frank, Dr Nanette,' Harry said quietly to the vet.

Harry led a stunned Georgia to the waiting room, sitting her on a chair. He collected Tru and carried him out to the car, settling him as comfortably as he could on a blanket in the back seat.

He returned for his wife, who hadn't moved an inch, and gently guided her to the car and strapped her into the passenger seat like a child.

She was still in shock, tears silently running down her cheeks. Harry reached into his pocket and handed her his big white handkerchief, which he always carried around with him. Georgia accepted it gratefully and blew her nose loudly as they drove away.

Back home at Carpenter's Cottage, Harry lit a roaring log fire and settled Tru in his basket, with Georgia alongside in her armchair, with a blanket tucking her in warmly. Her eyes were red and swollen, but she had no more tears to shed.

Her world had crashed.

INDIA

Alone in her study, Georgia pulled out all the veterinarian journals she subscribed to each month and pored over them: therapies, liver cancer in dogs, holistic treatment for dogs. She'd been at it awhile and didn't notice the hours slipping by. The morning sun was fading to early evening when something grabbed her interest: *Shaman, animal communicator and herbalist, specialises in holistic treatment of liver cancer in dogs.*

'Yes!' Georgia jumped up, startling Tru. She grabbed her hat and coat, blew a kiss to Tru, who nodded off again, and headed out the door for the local library.

'I won't be long,' she told him. 'Your dad will be home in ten minutes.'

At the local library, Georgia sat in the cosy reading room, books spread out before her under a reading lamp. One large book on holistic healing attracted her attention and she flicked through the pages until something caught her eye:

Animals, their forgotten language and how they can make you and the planet heal …

... Shamanic practice seeks healing and wisdom from realms that overlap the everyday world. The use of plant and animal medicines, vision quests, trance work and ceremonies to heal one's self and others are the foundations of shamanism.

India, especially, has a rich background of spiritual wisdom, which the western world is currently benefitting from.

... a shaman is a man or a woman who enters into an altered state of consciousness by using monotonous sounds like drumming, rattling or singing to access hidden information. They leave their body behind and their free soul travels into a parallel universe ...

Georgia was beside herself with excitement and read further:

Shamanism addresses all these spiritual causes of ill-health and recreates order and balance ...

'Voila,' she shouted, as she slammed the book shut. The librarian looked at her disapprovingly and pointed to the 'Silence Please' sign.

'Sorry,' she whispered and, grabbing her hat and coat, rushed out the door, driving home like a maniac. Fortunately, there were no traffic cops on the road, and she didn't have on her stilettos.

Harry arrived home to find a note on the kitchen table: 'Back in ten—G xx.'

Tru was fast asleep, warm and comfortable, curled up in his basket by the fire. Harry threw another log on, but didn't bother to turn on a light. He stared out the window, not looking at anything. The firelight danced shadows on his countenance.

Harry was worried, about his wife, his dog and his marriage; nothing in his experience had prepared him for what he feared was coming.

The next day, Georgia was on the telephone making flight bookings when Harry walked in the door and caught the tail-end of the conversation.

'I want a flight out of this evening to Bangalore, India. I'm taking my dog with me. He weighs fourteen kilos.'

'What the hell are you doing?' Harry demanded.

'Booking a flight. I'm taking Truman home to India to see the Shaman. No western medicine can help him. This is the only chance to save his life.'

'That's the craziest thing I ever heard,' Harry exploded.

'He's my son. I must do everything I can for him.'

'I love Tru too, but just taking off to India to see some witch doctor is madness!'

Harry was usually a quiet-spoken man, but this was all too much. They were growing apart before Tru took ill, but he had hoped that their love for the dog would bring them closer again. Now she was taking off by herself with Tru to the other end of the world.

Where did that leave him?

'He's a world-famous Shaman, with a huge success rate at treating animal illness, especially cancer in dogs.'

Fear mixed with anger engulfed him. 'No, Georgia. I forbid it.'

Georgia looked at him, surprised. He hadn't spoken to her in that tone of voice before.

'When you were thirteen years old, allopathic medicine gave up on you,' Georgia retorted. 'You were left to spend the last days of your life with your grandmother, as your mother had four other kids to look after. She sent for the witch doctor, as you call him. He saved your life with Ayurvedic herbs and treatments. Were you not given a chance at life?'

Harry just stared at her, concerned and very worried. 'I'll go with you.'

'You need to stay here. Keep an eye on the business for me. You can't leave your job indefinitely, and it could be weeks, months. Michelle will run the college with Lauren till I return. I'll call from time to time to see that things are running smoothly and keep managing things from there.'

Harry felt that this was about their marriage: Georgia was leaving; the dog came first. He was paralysed with fear.

'I still don't think it's a good idea.'

'I have to do something, Harry. I can't just sit here and wait for Tru to die. It's only a matter of time. I must go. I must try to save my dog's life—he's my son!'

'I'm your husband, Gi—'

'I know, but you're not DYING!' she interrupted.

'I might as well be. There's not much to live for,' he mumbled under his breath.

'Stop muttering! Speak up. What?'

A thick silence hung between them. Harry could feel the strength of her will. If only she still felt the same passionate love for him as she did for the dog. Or did she ever love him as much as he loved her? His anger evaporated and he felt flat.

'When do you leave?'

'Tonight on the 6:00 pm flight.'

He looked at her. In his face was the total acceptance of what must be. If he disagreed any further, he could lose his wife forever—a chance he was not prepared to take. He must let her go.

'When you let go, things change and shift and you gain what you never lost,' he whispered.

'What? You're always mumbling in your beard, Harry.'

'Nothing. I'll drive you to the airport.'

'I've called Sakena. She'll meet Tru and me at the other end.'

Sakena was Georgia's dear friend. She was a passionate dog lover and dedicated her life to looking after the lost and injured dogs on the streets of India.

At Canberra airport, Georgia checked Tru in at the pet terminal.

'It's an eleven-hour flight, Mrs Haines. I understand this dog is ill. All care will be taken, but the airline takes no responsibility for any adverse reactions or the condition of your dog on arrival.' The attendant shoved a consent form in front of her. 'Sign here.'

Georgia signed, making no comment. Harry kissed her goodbye on the cheek. He could find no more words. Feeling depleted, he waved a last goodbye as she disappeared through the boarding gates.

His heart was heavy as lead as he turned the key in the front door of Carpenter's Cottage. No Tru. No Georgia. Just silence.

He'd go down to the Lookout Farm this weekend. Some fresh country air and Mother Meg's cooking sounded good. Maybe call Jeff, his best friend and their solicitor, swing a couple of golf clubs down the Lakes Golf Club and catch a trout or two.

THE SHAMAN

'House of Secret Animal Business; Animals are Born Angels,' read the sign on the front door of an idyllic country house, nestled in a tropical garden. Bougainvillea cascaded over trellises, and the heady scent of frangipani, mingled with the exotic perfume of jasmine—'the star of the night'—filled the nostrils. There was a feeling of peace here.

Inside, sitting by a crackling fire, was a tall, strong, handsome man of Kashmir origin, a North Indian in his early forties. Tanned skin and piercing green eyes that seemed to penetrate one's very soul were fixed on the dancing flames. He was deep in thought as he puffed on a wooden pipe, a *hookah.*

He was the Shaman.

The room was small and cosy, with bright Indian-style rugs and blankets. Feathers, stones and crystals adorned the mantle. Floor-to-ceiling solid oak bookshelves dominated two of the walls. The scent of incense mingled with the strong woody aroma of pipe tobacco. There were cats and dogs draped all over the furniture. They were all compatible and in harmony with each other.

A gracious, dark-haired woman, about thirty-five years old, entered silently, gliding into the room on bare feet. The only sound was the jingling of the many gold bangles adorning the wrist of her right hand as she placed an earthenware mug of strong black coffee on a small table near the man.

'Master, you look tired,' she said. 'Do retire early tonight. You need rest. I'll feed the animals and settle them down for the night.'

The Shaman smiled at his sister, Serena.

'Thanks. I think I'll take your advice. I've just one more dog to see first. Mrs Clathrate and Jimmy should be here soon.'

Feet crunching on falling leaves set the dogs barking and a woman walked towards the house carrying a small dog.

'Good evening, Mrs Clathrate. Please come in.' Serena smiled as she greeted the woman and her dog, Jimmy. Mrs Clathrate looked anxious and clutched her dog closer.

'Hello, little Jim. How's my boy today?' the Shaman asked Jimmy, reaching down to pet him. The little dog lifted his head and looked pleased, wagging his tail.

'Jimmy's always happy to see you, Shaman.' Mrs Clathrate gave him a weak smile. The Shaman picked up the dog and took him to the window seat, settling him on his lap.

'Animals are extensions of God's love. Their purpose in life is to help us heal physically and emotionally. They are our mirrors and reflect back to us our own health and well-being. They love us unconditionally and will take on our ill-health and pain in an effort to heal us,' the Shaman said. 'Often this will make them extremely sick, and they suffer silently, even to the point of their own demise. We need to acknowledge this gift they try to impart to us, for their sake and ours, and the preservation of the planet.'

Mrs Clathrate looked at him with tears in her eyes.

'You mean my Jimmy's heart has taken on my anger and resentment.' A huge sob escaped her.

'Our unbridled emotions of anger, resentment, criticism and vindictiveness develop into ill-health, causing cancers, heart problems, liver and kidney disease,' the Shaman responded. 'The animals in our home try to take all these conditions on themselves in order to protect us. If we pay heed to the lessons they are trying to impart, of love and compassion, we can save them as well as ourselves from harm.'

The Shaman looked at her compassionately, resting a hand on her shoulder as Jimmy made small sounds of love. The dog would take on all his mistress's afflictions if it would help her. This is the unconditional love with which our animal companions reach out to us.

Bangalore Airport – India

'Hello, hello.' Sakena, a slim woman with long black hair in a plait down her back, enveloped Georgia in a bear hug and lifted up Tru, hugging him tightly and rubbing noses. Tru wagged happily, recognising a human with an affinity for animals.

'Come, my friend, I've the van waiting. All will be well. Tomorrow Tru will meet the Shaman.'

Sakena's home was charming. Dogs were scattered all over the place: a German shepherd, a golden retriever, a Labrador, a dachshund, two beagles and a little puppy of unrecognizable breed. They all looked healthy and happy, delighted to see Sakena, their mum, and jumping about and around her.

'Max, Candy, Tara … OK … Love you all.'

Picking up the little white puppy from his basket, she kissed the top of his head.

'What happened to his leg?' Georgia asked, looking at the bandaged hind leg.

'Angelo was rescued yesterday, hit by a motorbike. He had a lucky escape with only a fractured leg. He's doing well, the precious mite. Now, Tru can sleep here,' Sakena said, pointing to a camp bed set up warmly with a bright blue blanket.

The other dogs gathered round. One mother dog nudged Truman gently, taking him under her wing, with all the love of a mother for her sick child. Tru snuggled in happily and sighed; a sigh of contentment, feeling at home with members of his pack.

'Come, Georgia, my dear, I'll show you to your room. You must be tired.'

Sakena led Georgia to a small cosy bedroom. A large, comfy, well-worn brown leather armchair sat in one corner, scattered with red and gold brightly coloured cushions. The bed was turned down with a dark red quilt and looked warm and inviting. The large French windows and doors were open, leading to the veranda, where two cats sunned themselves in the afternoon sunlight. The garden was overgrown but magical, with large neem trees, roses and purple bougainvillea.

'Thank you,' Georgia said, hugging her friend warmly. 'I might take a walk. It's been a long flight and I'd like to stretch my legs. Tru seems well settled in.'

Tru raised an eyebrow and buried his head back in the blanket. Sakena nodded in assent, kissing her on the cheek. Dressed in sandals, a strapped top and long flowing skirt, Georgia looked the picture of grace and beauty as she stepped out into the warm afternoon sunlight. A gentle breeze blew softly through her long black tresses as she walked briskly down the quiet street towards the city.

'Rickshaw, ma'am,' called out an old turbaned rickshaw driver as he pedalled slowly alongside, hoping for a fare. She waved him a 'No' signal.

Two young sari-clad women, with fruit-laden baskets balanced on their heads and hips swaying seductively, passed her by, avidly engrossed in the conversation of the day.

'I won!' shouted a little five-year-old girl playing hopscotch with her sister, as she jumped the squares marked with chalk on the pavement, happy and smiling with the joy of carefree youth.

As she neared the city, she heard the noise of people singing and drums beating. It was *Holi*, the festival of colours.

With a senses of déjà vu, she remembered her last *Holi,* with Tics … A time that seemed so long ago now. Dancing in the streets with her first love, laughing and throwing clouds of colour at each other, ending up in each other's arms, kissing passionately, the uninhibited sexual atmosphere of other lovers fanning the flames of their passion.

'*Memsahib*, you have no colour … too white!' A child laughed.

The child splashed her with colour, bright red and gold powders. He giggled, running away. As she chased him down the street, picking up a bag of blue colour someone had dropped, other revellers call out, 'Hey, *memsahib, kaisa hai yeh lai lo*. How are you? Take this!'

They showered her with clouds of powder, blue, yellow and green. Giggling and ducking, she bumped headlong into a tall dark man.

'Steady on, young lady.' A pair of strong arms caught her, preventing her from falling.

'Oh, thank you.'

She mischievously splashed him with the blue powder. Laughing, she looked up into his face, and there was dead silence as their eyes meet.

Those penetrating green eyes met Georgia's, almost boring into her soul. Tongue-tied, she looked at that rugged, dark face and those unmistakable eyes.

For a moment, she was eighteen years old again, waiting for those arms to wrap around her in a passionate embrace. They were lost in a deep kiss, tearing at each other's clothes, their young, searing passion consuming them.

'It can't be … Is it you? Is it really you?' Georgia stuttered when she finally managed to speak. She almost collapsed as his strong arms steadied her.

'Yes, Georgia. And is it really you, after all these years?' Tics replied, leading her off the street.

'How … where …?' Georgia caught her breath, her mind whirling.

'Shush. Let's talk. Koshy's Café is around the corner.'

They sat across the table from each other at Koshy's Café, an old haunt, looking into one another's eyes, neither believing that the other was really there.

It was so surreal.

'We used to come here. It was our favourite place all those years ago. Now it seems like only yesterday,' Georgia said, somewhat recovered.

'It's good to see you, Georgia. You look well, more beautiful … A poised and elegant woman.'

Georgia burst out laughing. 'I don't look so elegant with *Holi* all over me.'

'We used to play *Holi.*'

'Yes.' She blushed, remembering the passion that followed.

'Still married? Must be. No man could ever let you go once they had you.'

'You did.' She looked straight into his eyes.

'I didn't know what to do at the time. I was young. Hollywood beckoned … I did get there. I tried to call and tell you I regretted my decision, but by then you had left Bombay. It was too late.'

'You could have written, said something. Not a word all these years,' Georgia replied vehemently.

'I did write to you, Georgia, at your parents' address in Bangalore. I thought you would have returned home. My letters came back "Not at this address". I didn't know where to find you …'

Suddenly, looking at his watch, he remembered an appointment, an important engagement he had to keep. The last thing he wanted to do was leave Georgia, the woman from his past, whom he had loved and lost.

'I've a particularly important three o'clock appointment I must keep. May I call you tomorrow,' Tics asked. 'Where are you staying, Georgia?'

Georgia gave him a long, hard look and got up from the table.

'How dare you take for granted I'll fall into your arms again, after all these years. Not a word! Goodbye!'

'Wait! I've just found you, Georgia. I must see you again,' Tics said, grabbing her arm.

Jerking away, Georgia walked off.

'Please wait! Let me explain!'

Georgia started running. If she didn't get away, she couldn't be responsible for her actions. He still had the power to stir something passionate deep inside her.

As she was swallowed up in the crowd of revellers, a group of teenagers surrounded Tics, showering him with buckets of coloured water. He was drenched and fell over, realising he had no hope of catching up with Georgia. His face filled with anguish as he remembered the feel of those voluptuous red lips on his, back when they were both totally lost in the moment.

The next morning, Tru was happily playing with the other dogs in the garden. Maya, the eighty-year-old *ayah,* tried to no avail to sweep the fallen leaves as the dogs kept scattering them in their play.

'*Chullo, Chullo* … Git,' she scolded, waving her broom.

Sakena was catching the morning sun, sitting with Angelo on the veranda until the puppy barked in delight and joined in the mayhem.

'Is this a normal day?' Georgia laughed. 'C'mon, Tru. Wish me luck, my friend!'

'Good luck, Georgia. The Shaman's a powerful healer. He'll help Tru,' Sakena assured her friend.

'Thanks for the loan of the van. Catch you later.'

The van cruised down the highway, leading out of the city, Tru hanging his head out of the window, sniffing the fresh country air with his long ears flying out behind him.

Cows grazed in the fields, a baby calf nuzzling and feeding from his mother's udder; horses, their brown velvet coats glistening in the morning sun, whinnied as the van drove by. The mist was thick as they travelled the narrow dirt road down into a valley, passing the sacred groves of coconut palms, and wound their way through meadows and past curious wild horses who looked up from their grazing. A bullock worked in the paddocks, pulling a bullock cart for his owner, preparing the rice paddy fields for planting.

'Let's stretch our legs, Tru.' Georgia let Tru out and he bounded off happily, delighted at all the wonderful new smells to explore. He had certainly picked up since arriving in India, Georgia thought hopefully.

'The Shaman must help him,' Georgia agonised. 'I'm pinning all my hopes on someone I don't even know, at the other end of the world. Well, we are here now.'

Tru lifted a leg and sprayed a tree. 'OK, let's go, Tru, or we'll be late.'

As they approached the Shaman's house, Georgia stopped to read the sign: House of Secret Animal Business; Animals Are Born Angels.

A feeling of peace enveloped her and she smiled to herself. 'We've come to the right place, Tru.'

Serena greeted Georgia and Tru at the front door.

'Come in, *Memsahib* Haines. It's nice meeting you. We've talked so much on the phone, I feel I know you,' Serena said with a smile. 'You've come a long way. And this must be Truman.'

At the sound of his name, Tru wagged his tail and made small loving sounds—a dog's way of saying 'hello.'

The mist had lifted, and the room was bright and sunny as Georgia sat by the bay window, with Tru at her feet, floppy ears splayed out on the floor.

Her mind was in a whirl. What had she done? Here she was, across the world, pinning all her hopes on the Shaman—the witch doctor, as Harry called him. He could very well be a fraud, Georgia thought. But he had a history of helping many sick animals. Well, now she was here. She was going to find out. Soon.

Trying to quell the butterflies in her stomach, Georgia reached down to stroke Tru, who was half dozing.

'Yap, yap, YAP!'

Tru jumped up as the Shaman entered the room. Georgia turned, her eyes hazy and a bit out of focus from the bright sunlight.

They stared at each other in disbelief, yet again, both speechless. The Shaman recovered first. 'We meet again. It's fate,' he said calmly.

'You … you're the Shaman? I … I didn't expect—'

'Sit down, Georgia. This must be Truman.'

Truman walked up to the Shaman, looking at him silently. The Shaman knelt down to Truman, resting his hand on the dog's head.

Truman was totally still. They remained so for a few minutes—healer and animal, bonding in a sacred energy that Georgia could almost feel.

'I've come a long way to find you, for the love of my dog,' Georgia whispered.

'And so it is written.'

'But you went to Hollywood … ?'

'We'll talk about that another time—soon. Now, Truman is of all importance, is he not?'

'Yes, he's the most important thing in my life,' Georgia said, collecting herself.

'Is your husband here as well?'

'No,' she replied shortly.

'I see. Let's have a chat with Truman. Come into the garden.'

The energy of this man in his Shaman role was powerful and strong. He led the way, Tru following after him, as Georgia lagged behind, her mind in a state of total confusion.

The gazebo was laden with breathtakingly beautiful and exotic flowers; vines of sweet-smelling jasmine formed the roof, and brightly coloured parrots sat on the neem tree that grew through the centre of the setting.

'What a paradise this is, Tics … Or should I call you Shaman?'

'I'll always be Tics to you.'

Tru sat at the Shaman's feet and waited. He felt the energy of the man and knew something important was happening.

The Shaman picked up papers from a table and read Tru's medical report.

'Truman has been diagnosed with liver cancer. One large tumour in the liver, but the liver is riddled with numerous cancer cells; secondaries developing is a matter of time,' he read aloud.

'Yes, Tru collapsed and nearly died. If it hadn't been for my husband …' Her voice trailed off. 'Please, please help him. I can't live without my dog. He's my life.'

Raising his hand in a gesture for silence, the Shaman started transferring thought telepathically from the dog.

After a silence of a few minutes, he spoke softly. 'The dog's been in a great deal of pain in Australia. It's been released since he arrived in India. Look at him—happy and at ease. Would a human, diagnosed with all this, look so peaceful and calm?'

Georgia's heart broke. 'Dogs are such compassionate beings. They're human … No, far better than humans. Truman's my son.'

'Do you have children, Georgia?'

Avoiding his eyes, Georgia whispered, 'I lost my baby boy at birth.'

A small voice piped up, '*Memsahib*, don't be sad. I'll find your little boy for you when I grow up. I will grow up, you know, and be like my uncle.'

A little boy about five years old entered the garden and went up to the Shaman.

He drew the child close.

'Come here, my boy. This is *Memsahib* Georgia, and this is Truman,' the Shaman said as he ruffled the little boy's hair. You could see it was a mutual admiration society.

'Ajit is my sister's son. He lives here with his mother.'

'There you are, young man.' Serena bustled into the garden. 'Don't disturb your uncle. He's busy now. Come and have your lunch.'

As Serena led her son off, Georgia had tears in her eyes. 'What a darling child,' she exclaimed.

The Shaman looked down at Tru, stroking him gently. 'Tell me about your life, Truman.'

Tru cocked his head and a telepathic communication seemed to commence, much to Georgia's amazement. She couldn't hear Tru speak, but felt the connection the dog had made with the great energy of this man.

Well, firstly, I love this family and they love me a lot. I was meant to be here, in this family, Tru told the Shaman very convincingly.

'What? Did you choose this mum and dad?'

No, silly, they chose me.

The Shaman gently asked, 'Did you get cancer to somehow help Georgia?'

I don't know why I got cancer, but I know I want to take her pain away. I'm an old dog now and I've had a dog's life here. It's been great. I've loved my life. Now the tail really started wagging.

Just tell them it's part of the Plan. It's part of the Big Plan, Tru said with a knowing look in his eyes.

The man's eyes filled with love and compassion. His lifelong love of animals, combined with his telepathic gift, had helped hundreds of people with their pets to understand and resolve behavioural, emotional and physical issues. His services had been used by zoos and animal parks in India and all over the world.

'When communicating with animals, I never cease to be amazed at how much they already know and the content of the information they share with me,' the Shaman said. 'Far from being unintelligent, they often have already come up with solutions we never even imagined. They are overly sensitive to our energy fields and pick up things that are still in our etheric body and have not yet manifested, such as heart disease and cancer. They tend to take on our anger, frustration and illness to heal and protect us. They are teachers and healers. If we understand them, we will realise we have an opportunity for personal and spiritual growth in our own lives.'

'Anger … What illness would that manifest, Tics … Shaman,' Georgia asked.

'The liver is the seat of anger,' was the startling reply.

'Oh, no!' Georgia dropped to her knees and hugged Tru, thinking of all the pent-up anger and arguments with her husband and parents, as she buried her face in Tru's fur.

In a small town two hundred and forty miles from Pokolbin, Matilda was captured, trapped in a cage, her wing feathers clipped.

'Well, pretty girl, you'll fly for me. This is your place now,' said a rasping voice, followed by a bearded, wizened face that frightened Mattie. She fluttered in agitation, hiding her beak under her wing.

Where was Percy? Would he come to rescue her? She felt so lost, so scared.

Harry rushed in from the garden, muddy boots leaving tracks on the kitchen floor. He grabbed the phone on its seventh ring, his heart skipping a beat as he thought, *Don't hang up!*

'Hello.'

'Hi,' said the voice he'd been waiting to hear.

Harry hoped Georgia couldn't hear the thudding of his heart over the phone.

'How're things going?' Georgia spoke cautiously, not sure of the reception from her husband. They carefully talked about life at home for a few moments before Georgia filled Harry in on Tru's condition.

'Tru's met the Shaman,' Georgia said. 'He likes him and he's doing well since we arrived in India. I think the Shaman can help him, Harry.'

'Take care, *buddhi.*'

'You haven't called me that for some time,' Georgia said softly.

'Come back as soon as you can,' he replied gruffly.

'Now remember to eat regular meals and take off your boots when you come in from the garden.'

Harry looked wryly down at his muddy boots and the tracks on the kitchen floor. 'Of course,' he said.

Where is Mattie? Somewhere captured, her wings clipped. Percy was so alone.

The pigeon sat on Harry's shoulder, pecking his ear, down at the farm in Pokolbin on the weekend. What was he trying to say?

We're in this together, mate, the bird seemed to be saying. *I'm here for you, as you are for me. Will they come home?*

'Love always knows the way home to where the heart lies. We'll just have to wait and see.' Harry stroked the little bird's head.

Georgia's mind was in a state of confusion. Tics was the Shaman, her long-lost love. Could she trust him now? She did then and look where it led her. But the years had passed and somehow he was different. Tics was able to communicate with her dog, and Tru was the most important thing in her life now.

And, damn it, he was still so good looking! Those hypnotic green eyes. Could she trust herself?

'Telephone, Georgia,' Sakena called out from the kitchen.

'Coming,' Georgia called as she hastily donned a robe, tying it at the waist. She hadn't got much sleep last night and had slept in this morning. Looking at the kitchen clock— 10:45 am—Georgia said, 'You should've woken me!'

'Fresh pot of coffee's on,' Sakena replied calmly as she stirred a large pot of rice and vegetables on the stove, food for the dogs. 'It's him.' Her voice changed to a whisper.

Raising her eyebrows, Georgia picked up the receiver. 'Hello?'

'I promised to call after my appointment! Lunch at Koshy's?' Tics' deep voice asked.

'Umm … oh … ah … I don't know.' Georgia struggled with an answer.

Sakena mouthed, 'Go!'

'Meet you there in an hour,' Georgia finally replied.

Not too sure her friend's advice was for her good, Georgia gave her a look, 'I'll be at Koshy's, if you need me. Thanks, *friend*!'

Tics sat by the window, not noticing Georgia's arrival, his dark skin, chiselled jaw and black curly hair etched in the afternoon sun. For a moment, she looked at him, her heart skipping a beat, wondering how he could still arouse her senses in a way she thought had gone long ago.

As he turned and waved, those green eyes met hers and her heart felt like a drum beating in her chest.

'Hi.' Tics pulled out a chair for her. 'I was hoping you'd come.'

'I didn't want to … Tics, we can't pick up where we left off. It was over ten years ago. I'm here for my dog, my son,' she whispered quickly, only half convinced herself.

'There's something I didn't tell you at the time. I'd like to now.'

'What could possibly matter now?' Georgia was a bit cross.

'Please, hear me out,' Tics pleaded. 'I was betrothed from incredibly young, bound by the custom of *sakar-guda*.'

'Heard about this tradition, but tell me more,' Georgia said, curious despite herself.

'In negotiating a marriage, the proposal comes from the boy's side,' Tics began. 'The parents of the boy go to the girl's house, along with some of the close relatives of both sexes, to give consent. If the boy's father is satisfied with the girl, he puts *haldi-gulal* on her forehead. The girl's parents then pay a return visit to the boy's house, followed by the same ritual, known as *lalgatu*. After a week of *lalgatuon*, the boy's father revisits the girl's house, with some close relatives, for the betrothal ceremony. He takes some gifts—like a sari, blouse and petticoat, along with some ornaments—to give the girl. Five women—*swasin*—put a *tika kumkum* mixed with rice on the girl's forehead. The bride price is also settled on the day.' Georgia was now engrossed in the story.

'I told you Mother was extremely sick and ailing at the time,' Tics said. 'I couldn't tell her I was not going to follow tradition and her wishes, especially after my dad died.'

'You mean you couldn't tell her you wanted to marry me,' Georgia said. 'Didn't I matter?'

'I loved my mother, Georgia. I couldn't break her heart, risk her getting worse. Do you think it was easy for me?' he asked. 'I thought leaving was the only thing to do at the time, the right thing.'

'Anyway, it's so much water under the bridge, Tics. Why are you telling me all this now?' Georgia frowned. 'And are you married to the woman you were betrothed to?'

'No, she died of cholera.'

'Did you achieve your ambition in Hollywood?'

'Tinsel Town fascinated me at first,' Tics admitted. 'I was cast in some bit-parts and finally landed a leading role in the TV series *The Bold and the Fascinating*. Ironically, I was engaged to a character named Georgia for the first part of the series. The writers then took her away to marry her first true love.'

Tic's eyes held the memory of a lost love. Georgia was uncomfortable, her emotions in turmoil.

'It's just a story,' Georgia said. 'Anything can happen in a story.'

'I wonder where the story went … I left the series and my life changed.'

'You gave up your acting career?'

'I became restless. Something was missing. I returned to Bangalore and studied under Yogi Ramaswami. Communication channels with animals opened up, the House of Secret Animal Business was born and is now my life and love. My second love …' his voice trailed off as his eyes searched hers.

Georgia, breathless, old passions rising, pushed her chair back hastily. 'Tics, I must go. I'm taking Truman home to Australia.'

'Georgia, please, I can help your dog. Please don't go!'

'Urgent phone call, *Memsahib*.' The young *chokra*, who cleaned up the tables, came dashing out. Tics thanked him, palming him a couple of shiny coins. The huge smile on his face was enough reward to warm even the hardest heart.

'Georgia, Tru's taken bad. I'm at the vet, Dr Ronan's surgery.'

'What? Where's the surgery?' Georgia panicked.

Tics took the phone out of her hand. 'We'll be there, Sakena. Let's go.' He firmly led a hysterical Georgia from the café.

'I don't have good news.' The young doctor looked at them seriously. 'The tumour on the liver has burst and surgery is required immediately. I can't promise to save your dog.'

'Operate immediately,' Georgia replied, without hesitation.

'These procedures are never cheap, Mrs Haines. Most people decide to put their dog down at this stage.'

'Never. He's in your capable hands, doctor. *Operate.*'

'As you wish.' Dr Ronan looked at Sakena shyly. He had saved many of her street dog's lives and they were good friends.

He was in love with her, but she didn't know it.

'C'mon, Georgia. It'll be hours before you can see Tru.' Sakena put an arm around her friend.

'I'm not leaving.'

'I'll stay with her,' Tics said.

'Thanks.' Sakena looked at him gratefully. 'I need to feed the animals.' She kissed Georgia, who gave her a watery smile.

Restless, Georgia paced up and down the waiting room, idly picking up a brochure from the reception desk. It read, 'Pets at Peace. We see to all your needs: burial, euthanasia, grief, urns.'

She dropped it, visibly upset. Tics replaced it on the counter, glancing at it briefly.

'Let's take a walk,' he said. Putting his arm around her, he led her out into the courtyard. She rested her head on his shoulder, sobs wrenching her body, which was shaking with grief. His arms enfolded her.

Was fate stepping in again?

Three hours later ...

A nurse stuck her head around the door. 'You can see Tru now, Mrs Haines.'

Georgia reached for Tics' hand and drew him with her, an unspoken message to accompany her.

Truman was lying on a cot with a drip attached to his front leg. He could still wag his tail slightly as he recognised his mum through the haze of the anaesthetic.

'All went well.' Dr Ronan entered, smiling. 'Truman is a little fighter. I've removed the tumour and part of the liver. He's very weak and must stay here quietly for a few days till he regains his strength.'

'Thank you, Dr Ronan,' Georgia said gratefully, kissing Tru.

At the House of Secret Animal Business, Tics, dressed in the traditional *Kurta-pyjama,* smoked his pipe, looking every inch the Shaman. Georgia was in an armchair at his side, wrapped in a colourful Indian blanket, sipping a steaming cup of hot vegetable soup Serena had brought her.

'Truman's a healer. Animals can reflect back to us what we need for our own healing and return to wholeness. Remember, how we interact with our animal companions, indeed with everyone, affects them and their behaviour. By acknowledging the good in others, showing appreciation and kindness, we raise their vibration.'

Georgia looked at him thoughtfully as she blew on her soup.

'You mean like a spiritual warrior, to make a difference, not with a sword, but with words and deeds.'

She reached out and grasped his hand. He covered it with his own. They looked at each other with love and understanding.

STOLEN

The next evening, Lauren was on the telephone from Canberra.

'What? Everything?' Georgia wondered if she had heard right.

'We came in this morning and everything had been wiped out, even the coffee cups in the kitchen, the filing cabinet—all gone.'

'Where did they break in,' Georgia asked when she finally managed to get her voice back.

'There's no sign of a break-in. The cops think it's an inside job, someone who has a key.'

'Who? All my staff have keys—'

'I think it was Michelle Stamford, the new make-up artist. Her husband owns a transport company. They've disappeared. Everything was moved in the early hours of the morning.'

'That bitch! I'll have her locked up!'

'Sergeant McAuliffe has just walked in,' Lauren interrupted.

'Put him on.'

'Good morning, ma'am,' the sergeant said brusquely.

'Good evening, here. Where is that woman? Have you caught her? I want all my stuff back, designer clothes …' Georgia was livid.

'Ma'am, it wasn't a break-in. The matter is out of our hands. You'll have to go through the civil courts. It's an internal business issue.'

'But—!' The line went dead.

'Damn!' Georgia slammed the phone down angrily and dropped into a chair, stunned. Picking it up again, after a few minutes, she dialled Harry's office number.

'Harry isn't in today, Mrs Haines,' was the infuriating reply—again.

It was the third time she'd tried to call Harry at Carpenter's Cottage and his office. Where was that man? Out bushwalking, instead of taking care of things at the college, she bet—just when she needed him.

'Tics is here.' Sakena poked her head around the kitchen door. Still annoyed at Harry, she greeted Tics abruptly.

'What's the matter,' Tics asked. 'Truman?'

'More business complications. Let's go and visit Tru.'

At the surgery, Tru was dozing in his hospital cot. Dr Ronan was attending to him, changing his dressings.

'Truman's recovering from surgery well. However, the pathology report isn't good. The cancer is spreading through the lymphatic system. I'm sorry. He can go home tomorrow. He'll be happier there.'

At least he was better. The cancer had been cut out of him. She'd leave the rest to the Shaman. Georgia didn't think she'd have faith in the man who once deserted her, but she did. The Shaman in him was powerful and profound. Tru was in good hands.

At the House of Secret Animal Business, a fire was burning brightly, dancing flames casting shadows, mingling with the candlelight from the two candles in small terracotta pots on the dining table. The table was set with a red silk table cloth, and banana leaves were laden with curries, vegetables, lentils and rice—traditional Indian style.

Georgia and Tics were seated across from one another. They looked relaxed. Serena entered with a bread basket, filled with the traditional Indian breads—*puris, nans* and *chapattis*—and placed it in the centre of the table. She had Ajit in tow.

'*Salaam, Memsahib.*' He grinned at Georgia.

'Hello, Ajit.'

'If you feel lonely without your son that you lost, you can borrow me sometimes, to talk to and play with.'

'Thank you, little man.' Georgia was touched.

His mother tweaked her son's ear. 'C'mon, Mr Charmer, it's way past your bedtime. I've put another log on the fire,' she called out, as she led her reluctant son away.

'Goodnight, sis,' the Shaman replied.

'Thanks.'

Georgia and Tics were alone. They sensed the charged energy, the high sexual tension arising between them, remembering their youth. Georgia had mixed feelings—the despair over her dog and her feelings of dormant passion arising for Tics.

He rose from his chair and moved over to the window. The full moon shone brightly, streaming through the window. Tics looked every part the Shaman: naked to the waist, a white *dhoti* draped traditional Indian style and tied between the legs. A necklace of beads and horn hung around his neck. Georgia looked bewitchingly seductive in a floating white strapped dress, touched with the traditional gold Indian *zari.*

Tics turned from the window, his eyes so intense they resembled glowing coals. Georgia could smell the scent of him, primal and raw. The shadows danced on his face, his body. Her heart pounded, sweeping her out of reality on a tidal wave of emotion, as if she was a young girl of eighteen again.

They'd been apart so long, any reaction to him should have died … she'd convinced herself. Tics had been part of her reckless youth, a part that had no ground in reality—certainly not in her future.

He moved towards Georgia and rested his hand on her hair, stroking it. She looked up at him and their gazes met and locked.

He drew her to him.

She melted into his arms. God, he was so sexy. Dark, dangerous, that sense of the untamed just barely suppressed below the surface.

She ran her fingers down his naked back. The movement was sweet and erotic. Tics slowly drew his fingers down over her face, gently caressing her forehead, her eyes, her lips. He seemed to undress her with his eyes. She was aware of her palpable fear and excitement as his lips moved down from behind her ears to her shoulders, her breasts.

He stroked her hair. 'Damn, you are so beautiful, Georgia.'

In his face was all the anguish of a lost love. Their lips meet, and they surrendered to all the passion of their remembered youth.

'Mrs Haines, we have tragic news.' On the line, the voice of the nurse from Dr Ronan's surgery was nervous.

'Tru … Noooo!' Georgia screamed.

'No, he was all right … I mean he *is* all right … I … ' the nurse stuttered.

'For god's sake, woman, what is it? Speak up,' Georgia exploded.

'Two dogs and a cat have been stolen. Tru's gone,' the nurse said. 'We think it was the man from the Animal Research Centre. The gardener recognised him as they drove away. He came to collect the specimens, we thought. We've called the police.'

'What animal research? Not my baby!' Georgia was distraught.

Just then, Tics walking in the door and overheard Georgia's exclamation. 'I know exactly where the Research Centre is. Let's go. I'll explain on the way.' Tics grabbed her arm, rushing her to his car.

At the reception of the Animal Research Centre, all was quiet. A middle-aged Indian woman emerged from the office.

'Can I help you?'

'You have my dog here,' Georgia said firmly.

'Madam, there are only dogs given to the centre here,' she replied calmly.

'I have reason to believe my dog was brought here. I demand to see the animals.'

'Sorry, that's not allowed without a permit.'

Just then a police car arrived, and an elderly pot-bellied cop entered.

'Thank god you're here. I want my dog back.'

The policeman, Tics and Georgia walked the rows of animal cages. The copper had a list of registered animals, ticking off names.

'Everything looks in order here,' he said.

Georgia was beside herself. 'But—'

'*Namaste*, madam.'

As they left, Georgia dropped her sunglasses on the floor.

'Expensive Diors. Can't lose them,' she said, returning to pick them up and quickly unlocking the bolt of a window in the room.

Tics looked at her in alarm, just as the cop turned around. Fortunately, he didn't notice anything amiss.

It was midnight. Tics and Georgia, with torchlight, entered the grounds. Georgia tried the window.

The latch gave and the window opened. They climbed through the small space and entered the room. All the dogs and cats were sleeping, most of them drugged. One beautiful large goose had escaped her cage and was wandering around.

They flashed the torchlight on each cage, looking for Truman, but there wasn't any sign of the dog.

A loud bark alerted the keeper and he walked through the area to inspect, shining his torch. Georgia and Tics crouched behind a cage in a dark corner. There was nowhere else to hide. As the keeper was about to flash his torch in the corner, the goose flew at him and attacked, biting him on the leg first, then his head, pulling his hair, causing him to fall over, and sending the torch flying.

Darkness.

Cursing, he tried to catch the bird but fell over empty cartons and landed headfirst in a sandbox of cat turd, sending a cat snarling. The guard passed out.

Georgia and Tics were turning to leave when Georgia discovered a door behind them. It was locked with a padlock through a heavy bolt. They looked at each other with the same idea. Creeping up to the keeper, they carefully removed the bunch of keys from his belt.

After a few trials ... bingo! A key turned in the lock and they entered a small operating room.

A dog lay on the operating table, drugged. A sign above it read: 9 am—vivisection cancer research.

Georgia gasped. 'Tics, quick, is it my baby?' They moved closer to the table. 'My son!'

Tics picked up the dog, wrapping him in his jacket, and they headed out of the room past the keeper, who was just beginning to stir groggily, holding his head.

The goose attacked, flying at him with full force, her wings flapping noisily. He put his hands up and stayed where he was. The big bird guarded him menacingly, while Georgia and Tics sneaked away with Truman.

They ran through the bushes to their car parked at the edge of the road and Tics laid Tru gently on the back seat. As he prepared to shut the door, he turned around to find ... the goose.

She jumped into the back seat, settling herself down comfortably next to Truman. Tics and Georgia looked at each other, smiling, and shut the door.

They drove away with Truman and Goose.

'What a turn of events! Now you must take it easy today—no more dramas for at least twenty-four hours. It's an order,' Sakena said.

The loud ring of the telephone broke through the silence of what promised to be a quiet, peaceful day.

'I'll get it.' Georgia picked up the receiver.

'Jeff Carter here.'

'Good morning, Jeff. That woman, have you found her? She'll pay for this … I'll ruin her.'

'It's not that simple, Georgia. Possession is nine tenths of the law.'

'What! She can just walk in and walk out with the whole show and you tell me she can get away with it?'

'Not exactly. Calm down.'

'What did that minx take me for?'

'My estimate of the stolen goods is ten mil and counting.'

'You mean it could be more? That bitch! Sue her!'

'We've located Michelle Stamford. She denies having anything to do with the missing stock and equipment. Until the goods can be found—traced to the suspect and they are arrested for the crime—nothing can be done.'

'I want you to slam her with a law suit.'

'I don't advise it,' Jeff said cautiously. 'She'd counter sue for defamation of character.'

'What?'

'When will you be back? I suggest sooner rather than later.'

'Truman is too sick to travel at the moment. Keep me posted, Jeff.'

Georgia's whole world seemed to be crashing around her … and her husband had gone on sabbatical.

'Come and sit with me on the veranda,' Sakena said, picking up the puppy and putting her arm around her friend's waist, leading her outside.

They sat in round-cushioned cane chairs in the afternoon sun. Georgia kicked off her sandals and curled up in her chair like a little girl, her arms enfolding her knees, resting her head on them.

They sat together in a comfortable silence, Truman curled up in his basket, enjoying the warmth of the sunshine on his back. The puppy clamoured for attention, so Georgia uncurled her legs and reached down to lift him into her lap.

'Life can change in an instant. Our animal companions never complain. They happily bear our burdens with unconditional love for us,' Sakena said softly.

'To the point of illness and even death. No, my Tru, I won't let you die.' Georgia buried her face in Angelo's sweet furry body.

A loud motorbike drove up the dirt road to the house, kicking up a cloud of dust.

'Aha … I wonder if it's Truman that brings the handsome doctor to our door, or something else.' Georgia looked at her friend mischievously.

'Hi, Ronan.' Sakena blushed.

'Hi, girls, how's my special patient?'

'Doing very well, if you mean Tru, thanks to a brilliant surgeon,' Georgia replied.

'Now don't give him a swollen head!' Sakena joshed.

Ronan only had eyes for Sakena. 'I was wondering … I mean, if you're free this evening, there's a good movie on at the local, and a food festival. Would you like to go?'

'I don't know. There's the animals to feed and—'

Georgia interrupted. 'Go on then. I'll feed and water the animals, so no excuses. Of course she accepts.'

Sakena looked at Georgia, half cross and half pleased. 'OK,' she agreed.

'Hop on. Let's go!' The young doctor was exhilarated.

'Is it safe on that contraption?' Sakena grimaced.

'Yes, ma'am. A royal carriage for your highness.'

Sakena sat side-saddle and hung on as Ronan accelerated and burned out of the driveway, happily whistling.

At the House of Secret Animal Business, Truman was lying on a mat on the floor in the classic pose dogs take, face between outstretched paws, as Goose affectionately pecked him. There was an affinity between these two creatures of nature.

Georgia and Tics strolled through the sanctuary that was the home to many sick and needy animals. Here the animals found love, care and respite from their cruel and traumatic past.

Tics had rescued thirty animals from the Research Centre, and they roamed freely through the grounds and shelters, putting together their shattered lives and finding peace under the powerful healing energy and care of the Shaman.

Georgia wasn't sure how he did it, but he had pulled a lot of red tape with the government, and probably handed over a great deal of money, to have the animals released and the centre closed down. He was a powerful man and highly respected.

Sakena thought he was the god of the animal world and often brought her rescued street dogs to him for spiritual healing, along with the physical love and care she showered on them.

All creatures have their time and mission in life, and when that is completed, they must leave. Many of Sakena's dogs had done just that and it was heartbreaking to her when they passed on, but this great spirit made it so much easier at the time of their transition. The animals were always so much at peace before they drew their last breath.

Goose was in amongst the three dogs from the centre. Like a mother hen, she was, as she pecked their ears, telling them they were safe here. They, in return, thanked her for being the catalyst in their rescue. Bird and dog were in complete harmony, as nature meant them to be.

'In the other world, tigers and lions roam alongside deer and goats; birds of prey with frogs, mice and lizards—all happy, all calm and compatible. No aggression. No dominance,' the Shaman said softly, reaching for Georgia's hand.

She looked up at him with her melting brown eyes. He could have drowned in them. She felt so at home, so balanced in this place, with this man.

'The dog must heal his soul. He has chosen to take on so much. Gemima understands.'

'Gemima?'

The Shaman smiled. 'Ajit named the goose.' He went on more seriously, 'The cancer has entered the dog's lungs. Lack of joy and resentment affects our lungs. We need to fully breathe in the joy of life each day.'

'Nothing matters except Tru. Please help him, Tics,' Georgia pleaded.

'Tonight, I will perform the ritual.'

Georgia moved to him, clasping her arms around his neck, resting her head against his. Gemima lifted her long neck and squawked happily.

THE RITUAL

Preparation was being made for the ritual. Serena and Sakena were lighting fires. They burned incense, laid out gongs, rattles, finger bells, stones and feathers.

The dogs were silently grouped around, watching. They knew rites were going to be performed to ensure the favour of the gods and other natural and supernatural forces—a healing ceremony for a member of their pack. They would silently assist the Shaman as he entered a trance-like state, to move into another dimension, to seek help in diagnosing and treating their animal friend.

Sakena brought Tru and laid him on his blanket in the centre. The dogs gathered around. Gemima stayed close to Tru. Georgia sat cross-legged on the ground, watching silently.

The Shaman entered a trance using drumming, as Sakena and Serena drummed along and rung finger bells in rhythm. As the energy intensified, healing herbs were thrown on the fires.

Georgia was caught up in the moment and joined in dance, moving seductively and with abandon around the Shaman as he lifted his arms in prayer to the full moon. The dogs howled. Gemima strutted around Truman.

The next day, Tru and Gemima were playfully pecking, squawking and barking. Georgia and Tics were in each other's arms.

'I feel different,' she whispered.

'Everything in our lives happens for a reason. We must learn the spiritual laws and follow them to the letter. When you do, then "magic" will be demonstrated in your life.' He gently stroked her long black hair.

'You mean feelings like blame, resentment and anger boomerang back to us and make us sick?'

'Our animal companions know this and try to take it all on themselves, to heal us.'

'They're angels.' She looked lovingly at Tru.

'We need to be responsible for our own healing, for our benefit and our animal companions. We create our lives from the way we think. Every thought and every word we speak creates our lives.'

Georgia reached up and kissed Tics on the cheek. 'I'm glad I came.'

He enfolded her in his arms. Where would this all end? Now that he'd found her again, he never wanted to let her go. But she was married to another man.

A good man.

Back in Canberra, Australia

'The biopsy results show a large malignant tumour on the liver; we need to operate immediately,' said Dr French.

Harry was in Canberra hospital with Jeff, his best friend, looking at him worriedly. 'That is unexpected,' Harry replied gruffly.

'Sorry, man!' Jeff clapped him on the shoulder.

'Shall I make the arrangements?' Dr French asked. 'We can operate this afternoon. I don't want to risk that tumour bursting.'

'Me and the dog,' Harry said wryly.

'Sorry?' Dr French asked.

'Make arrangements.'

Jeff looked at his friend with concern. 'Shall I call Georgia?'

'Hell, no! She has enough on her plate at the moment.'

'I'll be here, mate.'

After Jeff and the doctor left together, Harry asked the hospital switchboard to connect him to an overseas call in India from the telephone at his bedside.

Georgia was in Sakena's kitchen making a cup of tea and picked up the phone on its second ring, hoping it was her lost husband. She was terribly upset and irate with him by this time.

'Call from Canberra, Australia, for Mrs Haines,' the operator's voice rang in her ear. At last.

'This is Mrs Haines. Please connect.'

'Hello, Gigi.'

'Where on earth have you been? One guess—gone bush!' was the angry reply.

'I walked off the track for a few days,' Harry replied calmly.

'Just when I need you—'

'How's Tru?' Harry interrupted.

'Better today, but it's touch and go,' she replied. Then, feeling guilty, she asked, 'How are you?'

'Fine,' he said slowly.

Harry collapsed and the telephone receiver dropped from his hand.

'Harry, are you there?' Georgia heard monitor alarms and raised voices calling an emergency at the hospital.

Shock and alarm washed over her face. 'Hello … Hello?'

A young nurse picked up the phone. 'Hello?'

'What's going on? Where is he?' Georgia was beside herself.

'Oh, in the hospital. He's being rushed into surgery.'

'Surgery!' There was a dead silence as the nurse hung up. 'Hello … Hello?'

Frustrated, Georgia called Jeff at the solicitor's office.

The young receptionist, Miranda, answered. 'Jeff's at the hospital, Mrs Haines. Oh, hold on a minute, he's just walked in the door. I'll put him on.'

'Jeff Carter.'

'Jeff, what on earth is going on? Harry in hospital … surgery? Why didn't someone inform me?'

'Calm down. Harry's OK.'

'Harry just called me and then there was some sort of emergency. The nurse cut me off. I want to know the truth.'

'Harry has a tumour on the liver. He'll be operated on immediately,' Jeff came to the point.

'Sounded more than that. He seemed to have collapsed.'

'I've just run into the office to collect papers for tomorrow's court case. I'll dash back to the hospital.'

'Call me back immediately.' Georgia was distraught.

Jeff arrived at Harry's bedside to find it being stripped by a nurse.

'Mr Haines took bad and has been rushed into surgery; the tumour burst,' the nurse informed him.

Sakena kissed Georgia goodbye at Bangalore airport. 'Don't worry. Tru will be fine. Gemima will see to that.'

'Thank you, dear friend. I'll be back as soon as I can.'

The flight was long, but uneventful. As the Boeing 747 sped smoothly through the sky like a big bird that knew its way home, Georgia wondered: did she know her way home?

She was on the way back to Harry, her husband, the man she had asked to marry her. Had she been too impulsive? She felt she had lost her childhood, being locked up in boarding school all those years, feeling unwanted. Coming out at the age of seventeen and rejected again by her parents was a further blow. Did the lack of nurturing by a mother drive her to seek affection and throw herself at the man she married? Harry loved her unconditionally. She was the only one for him. But was he the only one for her? Had she done the right thing by both of them?

Where did her heart lie?

Tics was so damn sexy, so strong and had an affinity with her dog.

Two good men. So different, yet so much the same.

'Lunch, ma'am. The grilled fish or the Thai chicken curry?' The cheerful air stewardess' voice jolted her back from her reverie.

'Oh, chicken I think, thanks,' Georgia replied.

She wished all her decisions could be that simple, but that wasn't the way life was.

At Carpenter's Cottage, Harry was lying on the sofa, covered with Mother Meg's warm alpaca blanket, a steaming cup of vegetable soup in his hand.

'You didn't need to fly back, Gigi. I'll be fine.'

'I needed to see for myself. I never could trust you. You always say you're fine.' She smiled.

Georgia moved to the stove, to start preparing a meal, briefly ruffling her husband's thick head of hair as she passed by.

'How does your favourite lamb curry and rice sound, ~~baba?~~'

'Do you know *buddha* means old man?'

'And I'm an old *bhuddi*, so we make a good pair.'

They were comfortable with each other, feeling the warmth of the familiarity of their years together as husband and wife.

'I've removed the tumour and part of the liver, Harry,' Dr French said, looking at them over his horn-rimmed spectacles.

Harry and Georgia looked at each other with surprise. They'd heard this exact diagnosis before. Looking at the pathology report, the doctor added further, 'It doesn't look promising from the pathology tests. The malignancy has entered the lymphatics. You have about six months. Sorry.'

'Oh, god, what do we do now,' Georgia exclaimed.

'Chemotherapy. There's a fifty to sixty per cent chance of destroying the active cells. Choice is yours. I recommend we start immediately,' Dr French replied seriously.

Harry had a resigned look on his face. 'OK.'

GONG

Gong wasn't as spritely as he used to be.
Scully often raced ahead through the field, Gong slowly following now, with the aid of a walking stick, fashioned out of wenge wood and maple. The walking stick was the work of a master craftsman. Gong had made himself the stick when he crafted one for old Mrs Jamieson, who led the church choir.

Scully often raced back to his master, anxiously checking he was all right. When Gong patted him on the head reassuringly, he would bound off again after that elusive rabbit.

Georgia hadn't seen the familiar figure at the lathe, dog at his feet, burning the midnight oil in the workshop, for some time.

Leaving Harry to rest after a round of chemotherapy one afternoon, she took some of Mrs Jones' freshly baked gingerbread to Gong's workshop, where she found the old wood-turner rugged up, lying on the battered sofa.

'Are you OK, Gong?' Georgia asked anxiously. He looked weak and very pale.

'Just wearin' out a bit. Thought I'd take a wee nap.'

'You shouldn't work so hard, Gong. Take it a bit easier.'

'Want to get the pieces ready for the exhibition by autumn,' he muttered.

Putting on the kettle, Georgia brewed the old man a nice hot cup of tea and took it in to him with a thick slice of gingerbread.

As he gratefully sipped the tea, Georgia turned to admire his craftsmanship—a beautiful Tasmanian blackwood dining table and quilted raindrop-figured blackwood chairs, complemented with an exquisite sideboard of blackheart sassafras.

The heartwood is a creamy to light-grey colour and often has a black stain, which is caused by a bacterial infection. The blackheart was in great demand for turnery, and Gong had used it to perfection in the sideboard.

'How's married life treating you, young lady,' Gong asked.

'Couldn't be happier,' she smiled, noting how tired he looked. The old carpenter had grown very dear to her heart.

Scully looked at the uneaten gingerbread on his master's plate, ears cocked, sniffing expectantly. Laughing, Gong tossed it in the air, watching it disappear in one gulp.

The loud thumping of the Great Dane's tail on the wood floor said it all: *Thank you for the gingerbread, but, most of all, thank you for loving and caring for a great big silly like me.*

Gong's fingers, now curled with arthritis, stroked the dog's head. The feeling was mutual. 'Harry's a good man, one of the best. I know one when I see 'em,' Gong said softly.

'They lost the mould when they made you, Gong,' Georgia replied. 'Martha was a lucky woman.'

'She was my best friend. Remember to always keep friendship alive in your marriage, Georgia. It's important to be good friends. Talk about the day's happenings, about each other's goals and dreams, fears, everything, right down to the ache in your big toe,' Gong said. 'Share everything.

Your marriage will last a lifetime. Self-centredness is the main cause of marriage breakdown. Husband and wife should make each other their work of art and carve out a life together, supporting and nurturing one another to be the best they can be.'

Two days later, past midnight on a rainy night, there was a thunderous noise, as something almost crashed through Georgia's front door, shaking it to its foundations, followed by a loud howling.

Hastily Harry and Georgia donned robes to find Scully at the door. He was agitated and clearly wanted them to follow him, leading the way to the workshop. Georgia told Harry to stay home out of the rain, and raced after the dog.

Gong lay on the sofa, his face serene; but his spirit had left quietly, sometime during the night.

The morning of Gong's funeral dawned overcast and dreary. The day looked how Georgia felt, she thought as she walked down the aisle to the front pew. She was happy to see the many friends Gong and Scully had made filling the church. The pastor began his eulogy, a tribute to both Gong and the dog that had changed his life.

After the service, Georgia, with the Great Dane at her side, thanked the many people, young and old, that came to pay their respects to their friend, laid out in regal style in one of his own handmade caskets, hewn and carved out of prime burr walnut and solid ash. This unique casket was truly a work of art: hand-carved rose features were meticulously inlaid by Gong, and the coffin was finished in a stunning 'piano' gloss. Polished solid-brass contemporary hardware completed the exterior, and the interior was lined in a beautiful Italian designer ultra-suede.

He had named it 'The Last Supper'. When Georgia admired his workmanship and asked if it was for anyone in particular, he just replied, 'Someone who will need it to rest his weary bones soon.'

It was his gift to himself, and Georgia laid him to rest in his own masterpiece, thinking, 'Goodbye, dear man. Enjoy the big workshop in the sky, with your beautiful Martha at your side again. Scully and I will miss you more than you can ever know.'

Gong's exquisite works of art would live on in the homes of rich and famous and ordinary men around the world.

'A man of integrity and great talent, whose creations depicted the yearning of the soul,' said old Mrs Jones, as she came up to Scully, patting the dog on the head and handing him a piece of her gingerbread.

Scully drooled and gently accepted the gingerbread, softly padding to his master's casket with it in his mouth. There he gently laid it on the coffin over the inscription, 'The Last Supper'.

One loud 'ruff' said, *Thanks, Dad; love you.*

Back at Carpenter's Cottage, Scully laid his head in Georgia's lap. He knew she'd take care of him, even if he ate her out of house and home.

Georgia hugged the big fellow, noticing a small container attached to his collar. Opening it, she drew out a single sheet of paper. It was a letter addressed to her in old Gong's artistic handwriting.

Dear Georgia,

After Martha died, I lost the will to live; then you came along … and Scully. My life took on new meaning. I looked forward to each day again, the turning of the lathe, and made new friends that Scully introduced me to.

Thank you for making an old, lonely man happy, dear girl. The daughter Martha and I never had, I found in you.

I would like Carpenter's Cottage to be your home for as long as you wish. I bequeath it to you with much love.

Fondly,

Gong Browne.

FATHER

While waiting for Harry to finish a chemotherapy treatment at Canberra hospital one day, Georgia went to the coffee shop for a cup of coffee.

'Hello, Georgia. Haven't seen you for a while.' Georgia turned around to find one of her mother's society friends.

'Good morning, Mrs Hardcastle.'

'Shame about your father. Such a strong and powerful man to be struck down with that dreaded illness. Must be awfully hard on Marianne.'

Trying not to show she was taken by surprise, Georgia hurriedly paid for the coffee and bid her mother's friend goodbye. Did she hear right? Her father was sick, something terrible? Dr Martin, the family doctor, had his rooms in the hospital. She'd pop in and see if she could have a word with him.

'Enjoy a cappuccino, no sugar, on the house,' she said as she handed the coffee to a young woman sitting in the foyer, much to her surprise.

Dr Martin's waiting room was empty as she approached the receptionist. 'I need to see Dr Martin urgently,' she requested.

'Let's see … You're lucky, Mrs Haines. He's just come in and has a few minutes before his first patient. Go right in.'

'Good morning, Dr Martin,' Georgia greeted the kindly doctor.

'Hello, young lady; and what brings you here this morning?' the doctor asked. 'You look well.'

'It's not me, Dr Martin; it's my dad,' she replied.

'Aha … Jon … yes.'

'Can you explain a bit more about his case. I'm a bit confused,' she ventured hesitatingly.

'Well, it's only the early stages of dementia, but the mood and personality of people with Alzheimer's can change. They can become confused, suspicious, depressed, fearful or anxious. They may be easily upset at home, at work, with friends or in places where they are out of their comfort zone.'

'Does it get worse, Dr Martin?'

'Well, the reality is Alzheimer's disease has no survivors. It destroys brain cells and causes memory changes, erratic behaviours and loss of body functions. It slowly and painfully takes away a person's ability to connect with others, think, eat, talk, walk and find his or her way home.'

'Are there treatments available to stop the progression?'

'No, unfortunately, Georgia. Some things he may remember, some not. The long-term memory tends to be retained better than the short-term, but it's often fragmented. Don't be upset if he forgets who you are. It's difficult, I know, but all one can do is offer love and care at this time. Your mother has engaged a full-time nurse for him, I understand, but it must be exceedingly difficult for her. It always is for the other partner.'

'Thank you, Dr Martin, I understand better now,' Georgia said, trying not to look too shocked as her mind sought to grasp the information.

'Anytime, young lady. Give my regards to Marianne.'

Mother Meg had arrived to help out during Harry's treatments. Georgia settled Harry in with her and drove the thirty kilometres to her parents' home. She still had a key, but knocked on the front door instead. Sally, the maid, let her in.

'Hello, Mum.'

Marianne Hathaway looked up from the morning newspaper and the usual hardness in her eyes seemed to have changed to something Georgia couldn't quite decipher.

'Georgia, how are you?' she replied, far more softly than her usual strident tone.

'Dad … I spoke to Doc Martin … How is he?' Georgia was overwhelmed with feelings she couldn't express. She went up to her mother, and gave her a bear hug.

For the first time in Georgia's memory, Marianne Hathaway let her guard down and, resting her head on her daughter's shoulder, sobbed uncontrollably. When her tears subsided, Georgia said gently, 'You should have told me.'

Mother and daughter sat side by side, united in their grief for a father and husband.

'I love your father, more than you know. He's stood by me through all these years, providing for his family without complaint,' Marianne said. 'He's a good man in heart and soul, a leader in his professional life. Why did this happen to him, of all people?'

'I don't know, Mum.'

'Sometimes, I think it's my lot in life—my karma—to learn patience, to care for your father. The nurse helps with the domestic chores and his medical care. I won't put him in a home; this is his home, the beautiful house he built. He would have wanted to spend the last of his days here.'

Georgia kissed her on the cheek and Marianne rested her hand on her daughter's hair.

'You know, if there was one thing I could change, it would be not to have sent you away to boarding school all those years.'

Georgia, choked with emotion, just hugged her.

Returning the next morning, Georgia found her father at the breakfast table eating eggs and bacon. The eggs always had to be sunny-side-up and crispy around the edges. He carefully buttered the toast, topped it with marmalade, and sat an egg on top; he was on routine, doing what he had always done every morning.

Georgia noticed that something was different in his eyes.

Making formal small conversation at the table, as was the usual order of the day in her family, she asked, 'Would you like the morning paper? It has just arrived.'

He put his fork down and looked directly at his daughter.

'I woke up today and didn't know who I was,' Jon said. 'I know this because my wife told me. That's certainly part of Alzheimer's. You can't remember what you can't remember. At the end of the day, I say to myself, "I've got two choices here: I can mourn this illness, or I can celebrate life." I love my wife, I love my family, I love life. I'm going to live life to the fullest, as I always have.'

Georgia's eyes filled with tears, her heart breaking for the father who had always been such an indomitable person, a fighter pilot, an air marshal who commanded an air force, who had been President Sukarno's right-hand man.

Her mind was in turmoil. He accepted it. Could she? Then Jon asked, 'Who are you, beautiful woman?'

'Your daughter, Dad, Georgia.'

She rose and wiped a smear of egg off the edge of his lips. He smiled and put his arm around his daughter, holding her close.

In the months that followed, her father's illness progressed. While coping with Harry's treatments, Mother Meg's presence allowed Georgia to spend many hours at her parents' home, reading snippets of the newspaper to her dad, including—always—the stock market reports. He still wanted to know how his shares were faring and the Dow Jones index.

As the various stages of the illness manifested themselves, his reaction to it changed. Denial had been the first stage, but he had moved on to a desire for answers.

'Why is this happening to me?' he asked. 'Did I do something wrong?'

In the early stages, Jon's long-term memory was good. He talked a lot about his service in the Second World War. He served as a fighter pilot and dive bomber pilot in the India and Burma theatres of war during the Second World War. Georgia was so fascinated with his accounts of the war days, she started to write a journal. Father and daughter would spend many hours sitting in the sunshine by the crystal-clear pond, talking about his career, as frogs croaked and ducks swam around, bobbing their heads to gobble up a tasty morsel floating on the surface.

He had lost a lot of weight and was always cold, though the weather was turning warm and spring was just around the corner.

One day, as they sat by the pond, Jon—comfortably wrapped in a warm goat's hair blanket and beanie knitted by Harry's mum—was anxious to talk.

'My squadron was *The Twelve Apostles,* flying dive bombers and fighter pilots. I flew in both positions,' he said proudly.

'It was the devil's war: braving the Japanese sniper attacks, hostile weather and deadly serpents as Indian troops advanced slowly past Kohima and into Burma. Suddenly, war cries rent the air and Japanese soldiers leapt out of their hidden perches on the trees, digging their bayonets deep into the Indian Bravehearts led by the commandant, General Wingate.'

Jon gazed at the pond, but saw only the past.

'It was a perfect ambush,' he continued. 'Naked soldiers, their bodies camouflaged to match the colour of the bark of a tree, hid during the day and attacked by night. They came at the Indians like wasps stinging to kill. The Indians were novices in jungle warfare and fell like flies.

'Australians and Americans fought the same war, but were never the first line of defence, like the British officers. The Indian *Gorkha* and the *Jat* regiments were always on the frontline, *Kukris* against Japanese rifles. The *Gorkha* would leave the camp vowing to bring back a Japanese soldier's head. Their courage was unbelievable.

'The British army requisitioned flame throwers from England to flush out Japanese soldiers hiding in fox holes dug on the slopes of the Chindith Hills in Burma. Losses on the Indian side were heavy once the Japanese suicide squads were let loose on land, air and water in 1945.

'We flew Hurricanes, Spitfires and dive bombers. The Spitfires had eight guns on their wings and sometimes also a cannon. They were faster planes, flying at 500 kilometres per hour. I mainly flew the dive bomber. It carried one bomb on the undercarriage and one on the nose. In addition they had firing guns on the wings. To bomb a target we had to fly vertically and hit the target. Also, keeping vertical made it harder to be shot at. One of our squadron did not come out of the nosedive and, although he hit the target successfully, he was also a human target.

'The Japs put up double-edged steel fences in strategic places. If you flew too low, you would not live to tell the tale. One of our squadron had his plane sliced in two. We lost two good friends, pilots whose wings touched, and the two planes collided in mid-air. Both pilots died.

'Officers generally got two beers and one scotch per head rations each day. That night our boys demanded the deceased pilots' rations be given to them, saying, "They were good friends of ours and they wouldn't mind us having their rations." Death was a matter of fact. We didn't even think of dying. If it eventuated in the course of the day or night … Well, such was the fate of the war.'

Georgia flinched and was visibly moved and overwhelmed by her father's account of the war days.

'By early 1945, a wave hit the troops. There were rumours of liberation from British rule if the Allies won the war. Morale was high but defences were weak. Japan held Rangoon for a second time and then it happened—Hiroshima was bombed, and the war ended in August 1945. Jubilant troops fired their rifles in the air, danced and sang, and Sikhs, Hindus, Muslims, Christians heaped praises on their gods.'

Jon eventually stopped to catch a breath. He was in such high spirits, eyes wide with excitement and his voice animated, that Georgia did not like to interrupt him.

'Dad, I was only two years old at the time.'

'Yes, Georgie, and I was not given permission to attend your birth. At my request for three days leave, the wing commander retorted, "Do you not know there's a damn war on, and you want to go home for the birth of a child!"'

Dad sighed, looking tired, and stroked his moustache. 'Do you like my moustache, girl?'

'Yes, Dad; very handsome indeed.'

'You used to comb it when you were two years old and sometimes tie ribbons on the ends.' He smiled.

'Would you like me to comb it, Dad?'

'Yes.'

Jon rested his head against the back of his chair as Georgia gently combed and twirled his moustache. The years had turned the hairs white, but had not diminished its bushy growth.

He sighed with contentment, remembering days gone by, his days as a debonair bomber pilot in his Spitfire, sporting a bristling black handlebar moustache.

Georgia's heart filled with pride for this extraordinary, courageous man—her father.

GOODBYE

In between taking care of Harry and visiting her father, Georgia had to cope with the situation at the college.

Turning the key in the front door one morning, Georgia entered the bare premises. Walking through the deserted space, she picked up a single red stiletto and carried it with her. Bits and pieces of make-up, clothes and papers were scattered all over the floor.

Whoever had done this had known exactly what they wanted; it didn't have the markings of a random burglary.

She walked the long path—the gangplank—to her desk, now understanding how her young staff members must have felt. Reaching her desk, she rested the red shoe on the table. Memories flashed through her mind: setting up her college, Harry helping her to paint and move furniture; Truman running around and toppling over a paint can, covering himself with red paint that left him pink for a while, no matter how many times Georgia and Harry scrubbed him off in the bath.

It was a happy time: the students humming and chattering; a student outfitted by her classmates in an outrageously mismatched outfit; jetting to Paris, Milan and New York; Harry and Tru sitting by the fireside waiting for her to come home, excited when her key turned in the lock.

The telephone jolted Georgia out of memory lane.

'How're you doing, Georgia?' Jeff's voice was concerned.

'Not all that good.'

'The police haven't been able to trace the goods. Most of it has probably shipped to China by now,' Jeff said. 'Would you like me to proceed further? I've some ideas. We can meet today. Does eleven o'clock suit you?'

'No,' Georgia firmly replied.

'But we're talking millions here!'

'I'm dropping the case, Jeff. Please tie up the leases, all the loose ends. Thanks.' Georgia turned to find Lauren silently looking at her.

'Dropped by to check the premises before the lease-end tomorrow,' Lauren said. 'Did I hear right? Were you talking to Jeff?'

'Yes.'

'You mean …?'

'Anger and blame are going to do no good at this stage,' Georgia said. 'Boomerangs are already flying back at me.'

'Boomerangs?' Lauren was puzzled.

Georgia stood up from her huge director's chair and looked down wistfully at it for the last time.

'Please see to all the details to close the college, Lauren: staff wages and bonuses, and anything that needs to be completed with Jeff. Thank you.'

She picked up the red stiletto, and Lauren silently handed her the matching one she'd been hiding behind her back.

Georgia slipped them both on, strutting out proudly with a seductive catwalk style, singing 'I'm a Woman', by Peggy Lee:

… Get all dressed up, go out and swing till 4 am and then
Lay down at 5, jump up at 6, and start all over again
'Cause I'm a woman! W-O-M-A-N, I'll say it again …

Bangalore, India

At the House of Secret Animal Business, Jimmy and Mrs Clathrate were visiting the Shaman.

'I realised Jimmy is trying to help me release my feelings of anger and resentment. I've assured him, every day, of my love for him and the desire to change my ways of thinking. We're both doing well, Shaman.' Mrs Clathrate voiced her gratitude emotionally.

'Some of my best healing has been done through simply helping animals release their fears or concerns by listening to them. Jimmy and his mum will both be fine. Good luck,' the Shaman said kindly, stroking Jimmy.

Tru was lying in his basket, with Gemima snuggled close. Serena, Sakena, little Ajit and the animals were around the basket.

The Shaman raised his hands in prayer, calling on the spirits. 'Let's all join in the vision of "seeing" Truman healthy and help him become so if that is his will. The animals in our lives are mirrors reflecting back to us our thoughts and emotions, which cause us illness. Their illness is our lesson.'

Sakena and Serena applied herbs from a smoking earthenware plate. Ajit stood by the Shaman, solemnly joining in with the ringing of finger bells. Gemima lay her head on Tru's and pecked his ears affectionately, fanning her feathers gently.

Serena served everyone tea and *pakoras* and, as they sat around the kitchen table, Ajit and Gemima chased each other round the room. There was much playful yelling, squawking and barking.

'Georgia will be pleased to hear of her son's progress.' Sakena laughed at the chaos.

'When is she returning,' the Shaman asked, trying not to seem too anxious.

'Don't know. Her husband … her business … She has a lot to come to terms with.'

'The only constant thing in life is change,' the Shaman murmured.

Serena stopped tidying up in the kitchen for a moment, looking at her brother compassionately.

'Uggg … aaah,' Truman retched and splayed out, sending Gemima squawking and fluttering in alarm.

Harry had completed his round of treatment and was regaining strength when the call came in.

'Sakena called. Tru has had a severe relapse. I'm going back to Bangalore immediately, Harry. Will you be all right, or should I call Mother Meg?' Georgia said, distraught.

'I'll drive you to the airport, Gigi. Don't worry about me. I'll be fine.'

Harry and Jeff were sitting at the bar at O'Leary's, Jeff with a schooner of beer and Harry gloomily sipping a cup of coffee.

'What's the prognosis man?' Jeff asked.

'They said six months if I didn't take the treatments, but they don't know how much that has helped yet,' Harry said. 'Maybe it would be for the best.'

'Don't give up that easy, man,' Jeff replied, genuinely concerned. 'With chemo and the modern drugs they have today—'

'What for? My life is my wife. I'm not hers,' Harry responded despondently.

'Drink up, mate. Let's hit the Grand Final tomorrow. I've got two good seats.'

In Bangalore, Truman lay in his basket, not able to raise his head.

'Truman tells me it's his time, Georgia. His earth journey is at an end. His reason to help humans become better people and live in harmony on the planet is fulfilled.' The Shaman's voice was filled with intense compassion for the dog and the woman he loved.

'Tru, look how much I've learnt because of you. Look how far I've come. I need you,' Georgia begged.

Truman gazed up at her with love in his eyes and gently licked his mum's face as she bent down to him. He'd been waiting for her to return, knowing she would.

Slowly rising from his basket, he led Georgia into the gazebo in the garden. Gemima fluttered down from the bench. She knew.

It was peaceful here. Only the dog's tell-tale elevated breathing showed he was dying. It was a full moon, and its light illuminated the trees.

It was as if Georgia was now being guided by the dog towards understanding. As she received it, she remembered, 'Animals come into our lives to unlock our hearts and change our perceptions of life. To make our souls bloom.'

Georgia looked at Tru with the deepest love and compassion.

'Go now, Tru, my son. Thank you for the gift of your life, my angel.'

As she held her dog close, so close to her heart, Truman passed away peacefully. Gemima kissed them both, making small squawks of love.

The Shaman came up silently behind them, reciting, 'And so his spirit moves on from this earth, having fulfilled his purpose, returning to its home. He is a born angel.'

The shamanic death rites were performed.

Serena smudged the area with burning sage. The smoke was used to cleanse the body. The Shaman inhaled seven breaths of sacred tobacco from his pipe. After each of the seven inhales, he blew all the smoke into the dog's crown chakra so the spirit could ride the smoke to the heavens.

'Thank you for being my son, my Tru. You will live forever buried deep in my heart. Goodbye. I love you.' Georgia tenderly enfolded him in her arms, wrapping him in the sacred swaddling muslin cloth.

'I love you. I want to be with you,' Georgia said, looking into Tics' green eyes.

Tics was deeply in love with this woman, and he wanted to keep her with him forever. He had never stopped loving her. But the Shaman knew it could not be. There was a sad resignation in his face.

'There's nothing left,' Georgia said, as a huge sob wrenched her. 'My soul mate ... my business ... all gone!'

'There's your husband,' Tics said gently.

'I can't do this. I can't leave you.'

Tics held her close, never wanting to let her go again. He'd lost her once, but he knew it couldn't be. Once his lips found hers she was transported to another plane.

Tics was her soul mate and she could not deny the fact any more than she could her own breath. Georgia sought solace in her intense grief. Her lovemaking was intense and almost angry. Tics felt her pain and responded warmly and gently with his caresses. But there was almost a reverence in their lovemaking. They were as two spirits bound in time. Their love was strong. Their need to connect rose beyond their bodies and into their spirits, for which there was no earthly satisfaction.

As the sun rose the next morning, Georgia rubbed the sleep out of her eyes to find Gemima in her cage and her things neatly packed and labelled.

'I thought if I got your things together, whenever you decided to go, you'd be all ready,' Tics said softly.

'And what if I decide not to leave?'

Tics didn't know how to answer that question; it was an impossible question. There was a mixture of love and pain etched on his face as he reached out to the woman he adored.

'Leave me alone,' Georgia said curtly, turning away. There was an awkward silence for a moment.

'Georgia, please …' Tics reached out to embrace her again, but she reacted by beating him on the chest and pulling at his *kurta* as he tried to draw her close.

'No … no … You have no right to make this decision for me.'

Tics' heart was breaking as he finally managed to draw her close and enfold her in his arms. Georgia broke down and sobbed uncontrollably, her anger subsiding.

'I don't know any other way, Georgia, my love. Do you think this is easy for me?' Georgia was touched by the deep sincerity of his words.

'In life there are no accidents, Georgia; everything is for a reason. I look at you and I see Truman and I see Harry and, no matter what you decide about your husband, I just know this is right,' Tics said. 'You have moved from the "morning" to the "afternoon" of your life. You're only a thought away from creating your new life. It isn't here, and you know it.'

Georgia looked deeply into his eyes, still softly defiant.

'Then why did we find each other again,' she asked. 'What was all this about? You said you never stopped loving me.'

'Because we had to find each other again. We each needed to heal the wounds. I never stopped loving you, Georgia, all these years, and I never will. But the House of Secret Animal Business is my life now, and you have yours,' Tics said with conviction.

The simplicity of the truth hit Georgia with a bang.

She released herself from his arms and turned away, despondent. Realising the utter truth and inevitability of what he said, she shook her head sorrowfully.

Tics couldn't bear it and reached for her.

Georgia turned back into his arms and they held each other as if there was no tomorrow, knowing their connection would last forever. Their lives had been inexplicably changed by the love of a dog.

Sakena was waiting in the van. Tics puts Gemima's cage into the back of the van, covering it with a cloth. Gemima was going to Australia. Tics looked across the garden at Georgia standing alone, perfectly still, gazing out over the horizon, the only woman he had ever loved and still loved with every inch of his soul, with a deep sense of sorrow.

Tics approached Georgia from behind, stopping a few feet away. 'Georgia?'

Georgia didn't answer. It was as if she had found a place of peace within her heart at last … a place of knowing … a place of strength. As she turned to face him, she looked as if she knew what must be done. As she reached out to this special man, his welcoming arms enfolded her in an embrace. Tics' face was full of pain as she rested her head on his chest, tears streaming down her cheeks. This man was a great spirit, and he had brought her home.

Tics removed his healing shaman's necklace of crystal and earth-tone beads—tiger-eye, brown agate, jade, citrine, green agate and green river pearl—placing it gently around Georgia's neck. She touched it with reverence and smiled.

'Look after Tru, my love,' Georgia said, and climbed into the van.

Tics stood by Truman's grave in the garden near the gazebo, gazing at the plaque that read: *For the love of a dog*

... Truman, you will always live buried deep in my heart. Your Mum.

He bowed his head, moved by Georgia's growth in awareness. He hadn't wanted to say goodbye—he'd found her again, his first and only true love—and her spiritual growth was his only comfort.

The Shaman lifted his head and, with eyes to the heavens, raised his arms in gratitude to the Great White Spirit.

A large white butterfly flew overhead. It was Truman's spirit.

As the van left the House of Secret Animal Business, Georgia didn't look back. Her eyes were wet with tears, but no sobs escaped her.

She was deep in thought, missing Tics, remembering bumping into him at *Holi*, meeting him as the Shaman for the first time and, above all, his tender communication with her dog.

Truman's passing was difficult, but he'd made it sacred and helped her through it all, right to the end. She realised Tru had a mission … as all our pets do.

On the flight home, her thoughts turned to Harry, the man she was married to—whom she had asked to marry her.

'On the flight home, her thoughts turned to Harry, the man she was married to—whom she had asked to marry her.

He loved her with all his being she knew. But did she love him back in the same way? He was the kindest person on earth, and she would never hurt him. But there was something she still longed for, something her soul was still searching for. Would she ever find it?'

HOME

As the taxi pulled into the driveway of Carpenter's Cottage, Georgia's heart skipped a beat. No Tru bounding up the path to greet her; he'd never do that again.

He'd gone. Forever.

But wait … With a loud 'Woof, woof,' a huge beast hurled itself at her, almost knocking her off her feet.

'Scully, you great big hound.' She laughed, hugging the Great Dane.

'He's been waiting for you,' Harry's quiet voice greeted her as she looked up.

His wife was as beautiful as ever, but in a completely different way. Her whole demeanour was much softer: her clothes, the expression on her face; there was a calm centre to her, a softness and strength. The bossy business woman had gone.

Somewhere in India, she had found her true self.

Georgia smiled at her husband, as Gemima pecked him on the leg affectionately. 'Hi, Harry.'

'And who's this?'

'Gemima, Tru's friend.'

As they sat in silence over a cup of tea, Gemima inspected her new surroundings. Georgia was lost deep in thought. She looked up to find her husband staring at her.

'What was happening to Truman? I felt the dog was mirroring my illness,' Harry said.

'Animals can reflect back to us what we need for our own healing and return us to wholeness. Oh, Tru, you spoke to my heart, my son.' A sob wrenched her.

Harry put his arm around his wife. She rested her head on his shoulder. It felt comfortable and so right.

An overwhelming feeling of love enveloped her for the man who had stood steadfastly at her side, asking nothing for himself. He simply loved her unconditionally.

He spoke softly. 'I just thought, if I did everything right, was the best husband, if I could just be there for you, it wouldn't make a difference whether we loved each other the same or not. I wasn't asking for more. I told myself I didn't need more. I always knew I loved you, since the day I first kissed your lips. I felt lucky that such a vibrant, beautiful woman would want to be with a plain old fella like me.' He continued, 'The more I think about it, the more I realise how useless my life was before I met you.'

A song started playing on his mind, and before Georgia could say a word he spun her into his arms.

'I can fly higher than an eagle | For you are the wind beneath my wings,' he sang softly.

'Mmm … Bette Middler.' Georgia closed her eyes and leaned her head on his shoulder.

This is what her love reminds me of, thought Harry. They could do anything they dreamed together, as long as he had her. With her he felt powerful and free, capable of dealing with whatever hardships may come. Georgia hummed quietly while they danced slowly together. Harry softly sang the words that had a stronger meaning than ever before.

'I would be nothing without you | Did you ever know you are my hero? | You're everything I wish I could be.'

Georgia sighed and squeezed his hand tightly as they moved slowly in unison. Her throat was choked with tears and she was touched to the core. She loved her husband more than she ever knew. She laid her head on his strong chest and felt his strong arms hold her close, though he looked slightly puzzled.

'You're my lover and my friend, and no matter what life holds in store, I can handle it as long as I have you. I've come home … to my heart.'

As she looked up at him, Harry leaned closer to those voluptuous lips, just as he did that first time all those years ago playing the honeymoon game.

This time, as his lips met hers, the honeymoon had truly begun.

'I've your recent pathology results, Harry, and I can't understand it. They show no signs of the secondaries which appeared on the last test,' said Dr French, baffled. 'The CT scans are clear; there's no signs of the cancer.'

Georgia and Harry look at each other in wonder. 'Tru, my son …' Georgia murmured.

'Uh … what?' Dr French asked.

'Never mind.'

They left Dr French's surgery hand in hand. As they walked down the street, Harry suddenly turned a cartwheel and landed on one knee at her feet, much to the amusement of passers-by.

'Will you marry me?'

'What! Harry, get up, everyone is looking.'

By that time, an interested crowd had gathered, all waiting for her reply. Blushing, Georgia said, 'Yes!' The crowd cheered as, linking arms, they headed for home.

'We're already married, Harry. What on earth possessed you!'

'Well, it was you who asked me to marry you, remember? I thought it was my turn now. I'd like to have another wedding. What do you say?'

'Serious?' She looked incredulous, but pleased. Her staid, quiet husband wanted to marry her again, renew the wedding vows.

'Yes,' she said. 'I'd like that.'

As they walked in the front door of Carpenter's Cottage, Scully almost wiped them out with his enthusiastic greeting. He seemed to have taken it upon himself to keep company at their place and resist his urge to chase rabbits down the stream. He knew, as all dogs do, that she'd be missing Tru and wanted to be there for her.

Gemima wasn't so sure. Was he going to chomp her with one bite? He was so big. Was he really just a dog? She kept her distance on the top of the mantelpiece for now. The telephone rang, startling her, and she fluttered off outside. The garden was more her place. She felt at home there.

'Harry,' Papa Sean's foghorn voice boomed over the line. 'Dr French called. Mother and I are so happy, son. Bring Georgia down to the farm this weekend. We must celebrate.'

'Thanks, Dad.'

'By the way, Mattie came home.'

'My girl came home too,' Harry said softly.

That weekend they packed the car, took Scully and headed for Pokolbin and the Lookout Farm. Mother Meg had cooked a delicious lamb roast, country vegetables from the garden and pecan pie for dessert. They rode the train, chased each other through the burlap maze and sat by the pigeon pens with Mattie and Percy.

Harry pulled out Mattie's cut feathers carefully.

'Why are you doing that?' Georgia asked.

'So the new ones can grow again. She's a real survivor. Would have had to fly low, dodge cats and other animals, without her wing feathers.'

Percy and Mattie cooed and strutted, wrapping their necks around each other as pigeons do when they have been separated from their mate for a long time.

'Where have you been, Mattie?' Georgia whispered, stroking the little pigeon. 'Did you get lost like me? Never mind, we're both back. Love will *always* show you the way home, home to where the heart lies.'

ALZHEIMER'S

'No more headstands, Jon,' said Dr Martin on his last visit. 'Only shoulder stands.'

'Half your luck, Dad,' Georgia said. 'I'd be lucky to get a foot in the air at yoga—head or shoulder!'

Dad had always been in good shape, but as the disease progressed through its next stages, he became skin and bone. He was hostile, then confused and paranoid.

'Who are you?' he asked, looking at her curiously one day, as he had so many times before.

'Your daughter, Georgia, Dad.'

He looked at her blankly, not replying.

Showing him a picture of a handsome young pilot, pipe in the corner of his mouth and cap tilted at a rakish angle, she asked, 'Who's this, Dad?'

'Don't know … But he's damn good lookin'!'

'Sure is,' she replied, putting the faded photo away in her journal for another day. If that day ever came.

Sally was putting up the tree on Christmas Eve, decorating it with gold and silver balls and twinkling fairy lights, which made the tinsel glisten and shine.

Jon watched with a blank expression, until something about the tree triggered his vanishing memories and he became animated and excited.

'We were a motley crowd: English, Aussies, Yanks, Canadians and, of course Indians—the *No.8 Pursuits*. We took off against the Japs from Chowringhee Road in the heart of Calcutta and downed a couple of their Zeros, but we lost half the squadron,' Jon said. 'The three of us who survived raided Mingaladon in Burma on the eve of the Jap surrender and captured twenty-one Samurai swords for our squadron. I've still got mine; quite a valuable trophy. Go and get it, girl.'

She went up to her father's closet and carefully brought the sword down in its scabbard.

'Look! That's a Jap's blood,' Jon said, pointing to a large patch of rust near the tip.

'Careful, Dad,' Georgia said, sheathing the sword and manoeuvring it away from his hand.

He was on a roll now and became very animated.

'Those Japs were a very disciplined outfit, and they surrendered Mingaladon to just us three pilots without any opposition,' he said. 'Lord Louis Mountbatten, who was the supreme commander for South and Southeast Asia, visited us and gave us a rocket for flying to Mingaladon before the actual surrender. But his final au revoir was "Good show, chaps!" We presented him with one of the Samurai swords and the 3-Star Captain's cap.'

Sitting by Jon, Georgia held her father's hands. He seems to vaguely recognise his daughter … or did he? His world was now so different.

Georgia dropped a kiss on his head and left her parents' home with mixed feelings—but she felt she had finally come home.

In the last chapter of Jon's life, he lost the use of his legs and became pretty mellow and childlike.

Summer arrived and, late one afternoon, as he lay on the sofa in the drawing room with the sunshine flooding the room and warming his thin, emaciated body, Marianne asked, 'Cup of tea, Jon?'

He nodded and said, 'A *doodh peda*?'

He had a sweet tooth and a penchant for the little Indian sweetmeat, his favourite. 'One? Two? Three?' Marianne asked.

A vigorous shake of the head and a half smile was his response. Ten minutes later, when Marianne returned with the tray, he'd nodded off.

'Tea's going to get cold, Jon. Wake up, dear.'

Marianne laid the tray down, gently shaking his shoulder.

Jon had fallen asleep. Forever.

Precious memories frozen in time were all that were left to be treasured.

MOTHER

Marianne withdrew at first, and became somewhat of a recluse.

She and Jon had lived a lifetime together. She was a very private person and it was the only way she knew to deal with her grief.

Georgia paid her mother short visits over the months following her father's passing. Not much was said other than small talk, until one day Georgia found Marianne sitting by a window looking pensive.

'Hi, Mum. Brought you some of Mrs Jones' fresh gingerbread,' Georgia announced as she entered the drawing room.

'Sit down, Georgia.' Marianne turned to her daughter and said, 'I'd like to talk.'

Georgia pulled up a chair and her mother's story—the life and love of a woman Georgia didn't know very well—unfolded.

'My father was brought up by priests, as both his parents had died in the bubonic plague in Lucknow, India. They were a kind couple and were helping neighbours during the epidemic, when they succumbed to the dreadful sickness themselves,' Marianne said. 'Every morning at dawn, carts would rattle down the streets with the driver shouting, "Bring out your dead!" Bodies were thrown into the carts to be taken to enormous lime pits far out of the city and heaved into the lime. It was impossible to have individual funerals.

'My father had a happy life with the priests and went on to college. He later worked for a snooty, haw-haw newspaper—*The Englishman*. His column covered earthquakes, massacres, mutinies and epidemics, and his travels took him far and wide into unknown and dangerous territories.'

Georgia didn't say a word. She simply listened to her mother's history for the first time.

'My mother eventually persuaded him to give up his wandering job and settle down as a teacher of maths and geography,' Marianne continued.

'Mum was born in Mandalay, which was in those days a wealthy Raja's town. During World War II, the Japanese occupied Mandalay. The British secretly planned to bomb the town at dawn, but the Japs got wind of it and withdrew, leaving a ghost town of beautiful palaces to be destroyed.'

Georgia learned her grandfather was transferred to the Northwest Frontier as a Director of Posts and Telegraphs, where her mother spent her youth attending a good convent in Multan.

'The Northwest Frontier was wild and restless in those days,' Marianne said. 'The tribesmen from the hills would gallop down to the plains, plunder the shops, kill and ride back to the hills, with bags of food and a few women thrown over their saddles. One dark night, as a girlfriend and I were walking in the grounds of the convent, two tribesmen sprang out from the bushes and tried to grab us. We ran screaming back to our dormitories and just made it—or we would have been the ones on those saddles!'

Listening spellbound to the tales of her mother's childhood, Georgia smiled. 'What a history, Mum!'

'And I had another great adventure with your father … I miss him,' Marianne said. 'I'll tell you that story another time.'

Georgia thought this might be the window of opportunity she had been waiting for, a chance to talk to her mum about how she felt. Her mother had always intimidated her, but seemed to be softer and more approachable at the moment. Her whole life Georgia had felt abandoned by her mother. Marianne was cold and unfeeling towards her, her own daughter, but maybe this had something to do with the way her mother treated her. That her way to show affection and love was learnt from her relationship with her mother. Marianne rarely showed emotions. Georgia had assumed from a young age that her parents were embarrassed or regretful of her. Her mouth grew dry as the question formed on her tongue.

Hesitantly she said, 'Mum, I know you said the pain of having sent me to boarding school still weighs heavy on you.' She was still not sure whether she should broach the subject. 'You need to know … I understand.'

Marianne was initially surprised, but turned to her daughter with something in her eyes that Georgia had not seen before.

'Your father and I thought boarding school would give our precious daughter stability during all our moves to foreign places,' Marianne said. 'In hindsight, you must have felt we abandoned you.'

When her mother said the words, tears burned behind Georgia's eyes. *I was abandoned*, she thought. The memories were still so painful. All those nights staring at the ceiling, wondering if her parents ever regretted having her. Feeling she was unwanted and a burden to them. She was a grown woman now who had tried to learn to cope without that answer. Yet, looking at her mother now, there in front of her, Georgia felt no anger.

Georgia remembered that day at the station, waving goodbye to her parents, all those years ago, as if it were yesterday, and her inner child spoke from her heart.

'The little seven-year-old felt she must have done something wrong to be sent away; the sense of abandonment never left her,' Georgia said. 'It's ironic, Mum, that many people see me as having a privileged upbringing. I had a hard time coping with home sickness. I tried to keep a brave face, but my days ended with heartbreaking sobs into my pillow at night.'

Marianne looked out the window, not wanting Georgia to see the anguish in her eyes. She found it hard to express her feelings. She finally spoke, so softly Georgia could barely hear her.

'A seven-year-old doesn't have the intelligence or emotional maturity to deal with this sense of loss. I realise this now. I understand your feelings,' Marianne said sadly.

There it was. This was the mother Georgia knew. The cold and rigid emotions, with the scientific-like response. It was a type of emotional control Georgia would never understand. When it came to emotions, she and her mother were polar opposites. For this, Georgia felt relieved.

'Mum, the experience has had a life-long impact. I developed a "strategic survival" personality—outwardly always competent and confident, but within, private and insecure, especially about the most important thing in life … love,' Georgia said. 'I found it hard to accept that anyone could love me unconditionally: family, children, friends. I always tried to compensate with material offerings till one day my wise husband said, "You can't buy love, my dear." That was a turning point in my life, and I went to the other extreme: stopping gifting of any sort to family and friends. I have now found a balance and understanding of this.'

Marianne turned from the window to sit in Jon's favourite chair. She had been doing a lot of that lately; it seemed to comfort her. Georgia could still see the pain in her mother's eyes over the loss of her father. No matter how cold she may be, Marianne was suffering. She needed comfort as well. Marianne found comfort in Jon's chair. Yet that would not help in the long run. With Georgia there, she was not alone, and the pain was lessened. Her mother was beginning to show her vulnerability and that she was struggling.

'In those days, Georgia, for reasons of social division and class, society believed that to be educated within a good boarding school environment somehow gave our children a head start. It would build character and self-reliance.'

Georgia knew her mother was just trying to explain herself, but that was not what she wanted. She wanted the truth, the emotional truth, an apology of some sort. She had been a seven-year-old, lost to the world around her. That fear and loss had lasted for decades. If there was a way for the pain to stop, Georgia would go to any length. Even if that meant angering her mother for a moment or two. There had to be something that could prove to Georgia that her mother genuinely cared for her.

'Should a seven-year-old be self-reliant?' Georgia responded. 'I understand in those days children were brought up to respect and revere their parents. I was always overwhelmed by the rigid structure of life in boarding school and, when I did come home, cried out for love and attention. But I felt intimidated with more regimental rules and being chastised or cut-off when trying to express my feelings.'

Georgia remembered complaining during her first visit home that the older girls at school made her polish their shoes and clean their lockers. Father told her that was just the way it was. Even in the forces, they pulled rank.

But even after three years at school, she was still only ten years old and didn't understand all that stuff from the point of view of her air force dad. All she wanted was a hug.

At that age, Georgia needed the closeness and love of the family, especially her mother.

'We thought what we did was for our daughter's good.' Marianne looked pensive.

'I couldn't tell you how I felt,' Georgia said. 'Mother Bernadine told us we mustn't upset our parents by being upset ourselves.'

'We, as parents, also had to cope with letting our only child go, hoping that the decision was worth it,' Marianne said. 'We were trying to give you some stability while we moved between postings.'

But you didn't see the red-eyed battles against homesickness, Georgia thought. There were nights where she would beg for someone to take her away. No child should wish to disappear, just as no parent should let their child vanish from their lives. Georgia's mother tightly pinched her lips together. This was the most serious conversation they had ever had. Georgia had never brought up the past like this because she feared only more rejection. Her mother would try to explain it in a way that meant she was right. But the truth was there was no real winner. Something was clearly bothering Marianne, just as the abandonment bothered Georgia.

'The tears weren't all one-sided,' Marianne told her daughter. 'It was heart-rending for us. We were instructed by the nuns that our daughter would settle in better if we didn't phone or visit.'

'I would wait for that red-and-blue airmail envelope to arrive from Djakarta, Mum, addressed in your familiar handwriting. Sister Bernadine would call me to the office to present it to me personally. All the letters I wrote home were censored and I was never allowed to write anything that could be taken as "complaining" about my boarding school life.'

'Yes, Dad and I didn't realise that long-term happiness and stability were not founded by being sent away so young, being forced to be tough and independent.'

Then it happened. A single tear trickled down Marianne's cheek. It left a trail across her face, and Georgia turned her head to fight back her own. If her mother was finally crying, it was only because she could no longer hold it back. This was true feeling. The discussion was closed, and there was nothing else Georgia needed to know. Now she could see the care her mother had tried so hard to hide. Her mother was only defending their decision to continue convincing herself. Even if, back then, it was truly something they believed, now there was proof that leaving a child alone without love does no good. Georgia had finally gotten the answer she was looking for, an explanation.

Georgia couldn't bear her mother's heartache any longer. She sat on the edge of her father's old armchair and hugged her tightly.

'I completely understand now,' Georgia said. 'I love you both very much, Mum … And Dad, I know you're listening. Stroking your handlebar moustache.'

As mother and daughter found a new place of understanding and healing, Georgia felt closer to her mother than ever before.

RENEWAL

And so, as the autumn leaves began to fall, Georgia and Harry renewed their vows and were married … again.

Tanya was the maid of honour and Marianne Hathaway was at her daughter's wedding this time, wiping a tear from her eye. Since Jon's passing, she and her daughter had found a common ground at last.

Georgia looked ethereal in a flowing white dress of chiffon and silk, a red rose in her ebony hair.

'Will you take this man to be your husband, Georgia?' the minister began the ceremony.

'I will, with all my heart and soul, take you, Harry, to be my husband, my partner in life and my one true love. I will cherish our friendship and love you today, tomorrow and forever. I will trust you and respect you. I will laugh with you and cry with you. I will love you faithfully and unconditionally through the best and the worst, the difficult and the easy. Whatever may come, I promise I will always be there for you.'

Harry, her husband, the man of few words responded with: 'The best thing I ever did was to marry you. I have always loved you. You are the centre of my world, my best friend and my true partner. My wish is for us to continually grow through our love.'

Georgia touched the necklace of beads around her neck and silently gave thanks to the Shaman, a man of integrity and a great spirit who had brought her home.

Percy and Mattie sat on the window cooing. Scully, Nugget and Jib, the three dog pals, lay on the church steps wondering what the fuss was about again. Their friend Tru had gone to doggy heaven, but that was okay; it was the order of life. *Wonder if he has trout to chase and a sausage or two*, they asked each other, but they'd have to wait to get up there to find out.

Mother Meg kissed Georgia as she left the church.

'In marriage one is meant to fall in love many times ... always with the same person,' she said wisely.

'Love you,' Georgia whispered.

Then, turning to her own mother, she hugged her and said, 'The seven-year-old has come home, Mum.'

Percy and Mattie flew in to perch themselves on the bridal couple's shoulders. They knew that love *always* finds a way home.

Tanya summed it all up, after showering red rose petals on the happy couple and kissing Georgia. 'May the road rise up to meet you and may it be a lifelong one you walk together,' she said. 'Not in stilettos.'

In the months that followed, Marianne returned to India to live with her only spinster sister. There she felt comfortable and closer to the husband she had spent a lifetime with.

In Bangalore, Sakena and Ronan were married. Serena was the maid of honour and Ajit the ring bearer. The only guests were the animals, the female dogs with ribbons in their hair and the male dogs wearing black waistcoats with white collars.

The marriage celebrant was, of course, the Shaman, and the venue was the gazebo near Tru's grave. The Shaman raised his eyes to the heavens.

'Animals unlock our hearts and change our perceptions of life—they make our souls bloom. They are Born Angels.'

Today was Georgia's fifty-fifth birthday, and she and Harry had been married for thirty years.

It hadn't been a bed of roses, especially in their younger days, but they had now reached a compatibility and camaraderie in their fifties.

'You are part of me,' Harry said one day, surprising her. He was a good man, one of the best, but not a man of many words.

Her girlfriends envied her. Some had been married and divorced several times, or had never married but had many relationships and children by different men.

Georgia had Harry.

She had always felt she had the right key, but had tried to turn it in the wrong keyholes of life. He was always there, at every wrong door, to lead her back on the pathway of life. Stretching deliciously, she smiled.

All was well in her world.

Till her world turned upside down.

At the first ring of the telephone, Harvey, their five-year-old cocker spaniel whined. *Not a long conversation on the phone now*. His brown eyes said it all.

'Hi, Gigi. I'm feeling a bit low, tight in the chest and sweating.' Harry sounded very out of breath. She looked at the time: 6:30 am. Harry was away at a conference in Melbourne.

'Is it your asthma, Harry? Have you taken your puffer?'

'Seems a bit different, but don't worry. I've called the hotel reception for a doctor.'

She heard voices.

'What's happening?'

'They've sent an ambulance, silly people; paramedics and stretchers. What the hell are they thinking of!'

Georgia became alarmed. In the background, she heard a lot of hustle and bustle, and Harry was no longer on the phone.

'What's the matter,' she called, panic setting in.

A paramedic came on the line. 'Mrs Haines?'

'Yes … Yes.'

'We're taking your husband to emergency. He's having a heart attack. It's serious. I'm sorry.'

'Mrs Haines, you can go in now.' The nurse emerged from ICU, smiling at Georgia.

Georgia put the faded photograph of a young boy and girl, a lifetime ago, back in her purse.

She followed the nurse into ICU, where Harry was lying in his hospital bed with the sun streaming in, forming a halo around his head.

He always liked the sunshine and opened all the windows in the morning, before he pottered around his garden in his pyjamas, talking to his roses. The dogs in their lives were always at his side: Truman and Scully, then Henry and now Harvey, sniffing out the lizards. All the doggie sons, always loved, always cared for like one of the family, till they drew their last breath.

Scully had gone to be reunited with his master in the skies after a happy life chasing rabbits and swimming in the river, fetching the sticks that Georgia threw for him upstream.

Harry knew she could not live without a dog. Now she had Harvey. It was a couple of months after Henry, their last golden cocker spaniel, had died at the ripe old age of fifteen, when she had a dream.

A beautiful tan and black-and-white dog, of no particular breed, seemed to be calling to her. The dream ended with the shock of finding out it was a female dog, when she was looking for a male.

The next day, Georgia searched the centre's website and there she was. She called the centre and enquired about the little dog. The centre owner, Monika, was very uncompromising and short, but Georgia learned she really cared for the dogs that she had rescued with all the fervour of a mother. She was not going to allow them to be put in another situation of neglect like that from which she had rescued them. Hence the almost aggressive interrogation of prospective adoption candidates.

Monika knew Georgia's heart had been set on another male cocker spaniel, but there weren't any at the centre. After a long discussion, Monika had just about convinced Georgia to wait, when Georgia decided she did not want to 'shop'. She wanted to adopt now, and insisted on seeing the female dog from her dream.

The dog's foster carer, Jane, told her the dog's story.

Fuzzy came from an extremely abusive background. She needed a lot of care, which required funding—and no matter what, Fuzzy would not be ready for a new owner for a long time.

While Georgia was talking with Jane, the telephone rang. Jane answered it to learn that a four-year-old blue roan cocker spaniel had lost its owner to liver cancer and needed a new home.

The retired show dog was temporarily back with its breeder, but she had too many dogs and would not permanently keep a dog she couldn't show.

Georgia resisted going to meet the dog, whose colouring, down to the white streak on his forehead, was the same as Truman's. She didn't think she could bear to be reminded of him on a daily basis.

Harry had funded the care of Fuzzy, but persuaded Georgia to visit the breeder.

It was love at first sight, and Harvey came to live with them. Mother Meg said it was meant to be. He was Tru's soul brother.

FINALÉ

Now Harry's life hung by a thread. The letter still lay at the side of his bed, propped against the jug of water.

Kissing him on the forehead, she left him for a while to have a cup of coffee in the hospital coffee shop and grab a bite to eat.

'Call me immediately when he wakes,' she instructed the nurse at the front reception.

Harry opened his eyes a few moments later, reached for a drink and looked at the white envelope with his wife's handwriting with surprise.

As he read the letter from his wife—the first love letter he had ever received from her—his heart seemed to jumpstart. The blood coursed through his veins and the white pallor of his skin turned to a healthy pink.

When Georgia returned twenty minutes later Harry was asleep with the letter between his fingers. But the monitor was silent. He wore a peaceful look on his face and a gentle smile on his lips. A man content with the life he had lived and the woman he had loved.

The nurse and Doc Martin stood at his bedside. The kindly doctor put his arm around Georgia and said gently,

'A cardiac arrest can follow the first heart attack, my dear girl. I'm sorry.'

Never waste an opportunity to express love. It could be the last.

AUTHOR'S NOTE

… and so my story ends. My fingers on the keyboard slow to the last tap … tap … tap and I press: 'Print—Publisher's Format,' on my computer.

I hope my story opens the eyes and hearts of others. Mine are open. My heart sings. I have peace … and many more stories ringing around in my head to tell.

As this book went to print, my mother died. Mum read the book, though she didn't get to the final chapter; but I know the important parts reached her because I found this note:

I now understand, my girl.

I'm sorry … Dad and I love you, our precious first-born. Mum

That's all the seven-year-old has waited to hear.

I love you, Mum.

GLOSSARY

Anglo-Indian   The term Anglo-Indian refers to two groups of people: those with mixed Indian and British ancestry and people of British/English descent born or living in India.

Anna   An anna (or ānna) was a currency unit formerly used in British India, equal to $\frac{1}{16}$ of a rupee. It was subdivided into four (old) paisa or twelve pies (thus there were 192 pies in a rupee). When the rupee was decimalised and subdivided into 100 (new) paise, one anna was therefore equivalent to 6.25 paise.

Bhel Puri   Bhel Puri or bhelpuri is a savoury snack, originating from the Indian subcontinent, and is also a type of chaat. It is made of puffed rice, vegetables, and a tangy tamarind sauce. Bhel is often identified with the beaches of Mumbai, such as Chowpatty or Juhu.

Buddha   Buddhi is an affectionate term used by the Anglo-Indian people when referring to older men.

Buddhi   Buddhi is an affectionate term used by the Anglo-Indian people when referring to older women.

Cartwallah   Cartwallah; or Cart Wallah; or Cart Wala all refer to the person who works the cart. This term is a combination of two words: cart and wallah (wala). Cart is a vehicle with either two or four wheels, pulled by a horse or a person and used for carrying goods. Wallah is a person who works the cart. Cart wallah is a derivation from the term punkah wallah. A punkah is a type of ceiling fan used in the Indian subcontinent before the electric fan. Wallah was the title given to the servant who worked the fan.

Chaat
Chaat is a term describing savoury snacks, typically served at road-side tracks from stalls or food carts in India and some parts of Pakistan.

Cutlet
The term 'cutlet' was affectionately used by the Anglo-Indian people to refer to a person who does not measure up to expectations.

Doodh Peda
Doodh peda is the term given to a popular Indian sweet made from milk (doodh = milk; peda = sweet).

Haldi-Gulal
Haldi is often used to refer to turmeric in Hindi. Gulal is the traditional name given to the coloured powders used for Hindu rituals, in particular the Holi festival.

Holi
Holi is a popular ancient Hindu festival, also known as the Indian 'festival of spring', the 'festival of colours', or the 'festival of love'. The festival signifies the victory of good over evil.

Hookah
Hookah is an oriental tobacco pipe with a long, flexible tube which draws the smoke through water contained in a bowl.

Lalgatu
Lalgatu is the term given to the ritual performed in India by the parents of both the boy (bridegroom) and the girl (bride) to assess and consent to a proposal of marriage.

Memsahib
Is often used as a respectful form of address for a woman of high social status living in India,

	e.g. the wife of a senior air force officer in India.
Pakoras	Pakora, also called pikora, pakoda, pakodi, fakkura, bhajiya, bhajji, bhaji or ponako, is a fried snack, originating from South Asia. It is a popular snack across the Indian subcontinent, where it is served in restaurants and sold by street vendors.
Pani Puri	Pani puri or panipuri or phuchka is a type of snack that originated in the Indian subcontinent. It consists of a round or ball-shaped hollow puri (deep-fat fried bread made from unleavened whole-wheat flour), filled with a mixture of flavoured water, tamarind chutney, chili, chaat masala (spice), potato, onion, or chickpeas. Pani is the term for water.
Rupee	The Indian rupee is the official currency of India. The rupee is subdivided into 100 paise.
Shaman	Shaman is a term given to a person regarded as having access to, and influence in, the world of good and evil spirits, especially among some people in India. Typically such people are believed to practise rituals and practice divination and healing.
Ya or Yaa men	Ya or Yaa men is a term used by the Anglo-Indian people to signify agreeance, i.e. 'yes' or 'yes, man'.

ABOUT THE AUTHOR

Stephanie Marie Roberts writes children's books and romance. She is a Book Excellence Literary Award Winner and Silver Medallist for *Joshua's World* and *Liam Shark Boy*. She started writing for her little grandsons Joshua and Liam, which grew into writing for all the kids of the world!

Stephanie is also an incurable romantic. She was born in India in post Second World War days when children were seen but not heard, to parents of Anglo-Indian origin. Her father served as a dive bomber and fighter pilot in the India and Burma theatres of war during the Second World War. She has just released a heart-warming historic romance novel 'Always' based on true incidents from her life.

Two beautifully illustrated books: a coffee table book of inspirations *When Love Finds You* and her heart book *The Well of True Gestures* help couples bond in their relationship.

Stephanie lives on the beautiful Central Coast of Australia with her retired secret-service husband Chris and sixteen-year-old pampered Cocker Spaniel Harvey. Dogs are her passion, and she must have a dog under her feet when she writes.

~

Manufactured by Amazon.ca
Bolton, ON